"Have You Ever Kissed a Girl?"

I asked him suddenly, feeling bold and mischievous.

Jimmy grinned. "Yes, I've kissed girls. Why do you ask?" He made a gesture toward the sky and woods. "You think this romantic setting calls for making out?"

I don't know if he saw me flush in the dark. "No, you stinker, I don't think it calls for anything." I turned to walk away when he grabbed me and swung me around toward him. He kissed me hard and long and a little roughly.

"Is that better?" he asked, holding my face between his hands. . . .

Books by Hila Colman

CLAUDIA, WHERE ARE YOU?
CONFESSION OF A STORYTELLER
DIARY OF A FRANTIC KID SISTER
DON'T TELL ME THAT YOU LOVE ME
A FRAGILE LOVE
  (*former title*, ACCIDENT)
NOBODY HAS TO BE A KID FOREVER
TELL ME NO LIES
TRIANGLE OF LOVE
WHAT'S THE MATTER WITH THE DOBSONS?

Available from ARCHWAY paperbacks

Don't Tell Me
That You Love Me

Hila Colman

AN ARCHWAY PAPERBACK
Published by POCKET BOOKS • NEW YORK

AN ARCHWAY PAPERBACK *Original*

An Archway Paperback published by
POCKET BOOKS, a division of Simon & Schuster, Inc.
1230 Avenue of the Americas, New York, N.Y. 10020

Copyright © 1983 by Hila Colman

ISBN: 0-671-60715-4

First Archway Paperback printing June, 1983

10 9 8 7 6 5 4

AN ARCHWAY PAPERBACK and colophon are trademarks of Simon & Schuster, Inc.

Printed in the U.S.A.

IL 7+

This is for Jesse boy,
Welcome to the clan

Don't Tell Me
That You Love Me

Chapter One

THE LAST PLACE I EVER EXPECTED TO FEEL uncomfortable was in our own family room in my own house. But there I was, perched on a stool, halfheartedly practicing on my recorder, wanting to be a million miles away, and feeling like some outsider who didn't belong. I couldn't believe what I was watching. It was unreal.

On the surface I suppose it looked ordinary enough: my mother, dressed in a new red silk dress with ruffles—I have to admit she looked pretty—and arranging spring flowers on the dining-room table. She had already put out her best silver candlesticks and good china and polished my grandmother's flat silver tableware. Now she was checking it all out again, making sure each napkin, not paper ones for this meal, was in exactly the right place. To say

1

she was nervous was the understatement of the year.

"You'd think the king of England was coming," I said.

My mom jumped. I hadn't turned on the lights, but she certainly knew I was there behind her since I had been making some sounds on the recorder.

"You startled me. I wouldn't fuss for the king. Besides they have a queen. Anyway, this is more important."

She gave me a weak smile, which was not like her. But then she'd been different for a few months now, not having the kind of wow laugh she usually had.

"I wish I knew why. How can you be making such a fuss about his coming home? I don't see how you can have him come home at all."

Mom made a gesture which meant for me to shut up. "Please, Melissa, don't start that again. I told you, the past is the past, and I don't want to talk about it ever again. If I can forget it, you certainly can. I want this to be a beautiful evening. What time is it?"

I looked at my watch. "Almost six. He won't be here for another hour. If he comes on time," I added meanly.

I felt mean. I couldn't understand how my mother could be so happy about my father coming home, or even *why* she wanted him to come. I had my own problem about my feelings for him. To tell the truth, I thought he was rotten, plain and simple. I know that's a terrible way to think about your own father, but that's the way he had behaved and there was no getting around it.

I hadn't always felt that way. Three months ago, before he left home, I had thought he was OK. He works in a planning agency, and he's very into conservation—saving wetlands and farmland and all that stuff that I'm for. In that area we got along pretty decently. But we didn't get along so well starting about a year ago, when I was fourteen and began to have boyfriends. He said he didn't like me to go with just one boy; I was too young. And I said that was none of his business. We had quite a few fights about that. But he can't say anything to me now, not after what he did. He hasn't got a right to even open his mouth.

Three months ago he left home because he thought he was in love with Marilyn Craig, my mother's friend who was divorced. Poor Mom. She was shocked out of her mind. She'd never suspected a thing. She knew Marilyn had been working with Dad because she was active in a group trying to keep a developer from putting up houses on some wetlands. I had noticed Dad bringing up Marilyn's name pretty often in his conversation at night when he told us what was happening, but I'd thought she was a neat lady.

3

I'll never forget the night Dad told me he was leaving. It was after Christmas. When I think of it I start boiling. He must have known all through Christmas that he was going to leave, but he'd acted just like always. He'd had presents for me: new skis, records, and a marvelous Irish wool sweater; and presents for Mom: a velour lounging robe and a gold chain and some books. How could he be so two-faced?

Anyway it was just at the end of Christmas vacation, the night before school started, that Dad came up to my room and said he wanted to talk to me. I expected another lecture on his favorite subject—that he didn't want me to go steady with anyone; I was too young. If I followed his advice I'd have nobody, so I didn't pay much attention. His face looked very serious when he sat down on the chair by my desk. I sprawled on the bed.

"I hope what I have to tell you won't upset you," he started off. Famous words. Did he think I was going to act as though he were going to Boston for a business trip?

"I'm not going to beat around the bush," he said, nervously pulling on the stem of his pipe. "You're a big girl now; fifteen is no longer a baby, and I'm going to give it to you straight. I'm leaving your mother for a while. We're not getting divorced, just separating for the time being. I have some things I have to figure out.

4

They have nothing to do with you; you and I will see each other a lot. I won't be far away. I've taken a room over at the Homestead and you'll be coming to spend some weekends with me and we'll have dinner together once or twice during the week." He looked at me from under his bushy eyebrows, and his eyes were anxious.

I was stunned. "Does Mom know?" It was a dumb question, but it was the first thing that came to my mind.

He smiled a little. "Yes, darling, your mother knows. We've talked about this and come to an agreement."

"What kind of things do you have to figure out?"

Dad got up and started to pace up and down my room. He emptied his pipe into my waste-basket and sat down to fill it again. He let out a deep sigh. "Well, I said I'd level with you and I will. Please try to understand, and don't get angry with me. I think I'm in love with another woman." He turned to me with a tense, drawn face. "This hasn't been an easy decision, and I may regret it. You're old enough to understand." He gave me that half smile again. "I love your mother. I will always love her, but it's a different kind of love from what I feel now for someone else." He must have seen a look of horror on my face, because his voice and his face became pleading. "Melissa, my

5

darling, this is the hardest thing I've ever done in my whole life. I didn't plan it this way. But I'm not perfect. I'm a very ordinary man. I didn't *want* to fall in love; I wasn't out looking for anything. But it happened. It's pretty marvelous and I can't quite believe it myself yet. I didn't want to hurt your mother, but she's strong, and a very attractive woman. Maybe she'll be better off without me."

I just sat on my bed and stared at him. Was this my father telling me all this, sitting in front of me looking like some kid ashamed to admit he'd stolen his mother's milk money? I couldn't believe this was my father, Sam Underwood, the big-shot planner. I'd admired him so, been so proud when he'd got up at town meetings and made terrific speeches, or when he was on the local TV news explaining why he was against changing the zoning laws to make it easier for developers. Here he was, looking anxious and sheepish, telling me all this rot about being in love with someone and at the same time, how much he loved my mother. Had he gone nuts, or had I?

"Who are you in love with?" I finally asked.

He got up and walked around some more. "I guess you may as well know. You'll know sooner or later. Marilyn Craig." He said her name as if it was burning his mouth.

"Mrs. Craig!" I shrieked. "She's a friend of Mom's. She was over here only a few weeks ago bringing Mom some tulip bulbs. How could she? How could she walk into this house? That little————." I had muttered a vulgar word under my breath.

"Don't," my father said sharply. "I don't want to hear you talk that way."

I looked at him defiantly. "You're not going to be here to hear me talk at all," I said coldly.

My father sighed and sat down again. "Don't make this harder than it is. Please."

"What did you expect? Did you think I'd be overjoyed to know that my father is running off with one of my mother's best friends?"

"I'm not running off. These things happen." He looked as if he might cry. For a minute I was tempted to put my arms around him, but I shrank back. I thought of Marilyn Craig coming in all bouncy and cheerful with those tulip bulbs, and I wanted to do something violent. I had even admired her purple skirt and purple stockings. Her hair had been black and shiny, and she had looked radiant in a low-cut peasant blouse. I wished I had kicked her hard.

"What time is it?" Mom interrupted my thoughts. She was still fussing around the dinner table.

"Only a quarter past six," I told her.

"Does this dress look all right? Maybe it's too dressed up. You think I should change into slacks and a shirt?"

I felt sorry for her. She looked scared, the

way I'd felt the first time I'd gone to the movies alone with a boy. "You look pretty. But maybe you'll feel more comfortable in slacks. I don't think it'll make any difference."

"What do you mean by that?" She looked at me nervously.

"I don't know. Just that it won't make any difference. He's not coming home because of what you're wearing."

Mom frowned. "I'm going to change into slacks." She went upstairs, and I sat and stared into space.

He came early. Instead of seven, as he had said, it was only twenty to when he opened the front door. I don't know why I was surprised he still had a key. "Hello, anybody home?" It was what he always said when he came in.

He came through the front living rooms into the family and dining rooms in back where I was. He had a big bunch of flowers in his hand. I stood up and he stopped and looked at me. "I think you've grown in these few months." He put down the flowers on a chair and held out his arms. "Am I allowed to hug you?" He was smiling, but his eyes were searching my face.

I shrugged. He came and put his arms around me. I didn't push him away, but I didn't hug him back either.

"Where's your mother?"

"She's upstairs. You got here early. I'll go get her."

"No, I'll go." He looked at me for a few seconds. "I missed you."

"That wasn't my fault."

My dad bit his lip. "You're the one who wouldn't come to see me."

"You're the one who went away."

"Aren't you ever going to forgive me?"

"I don't know."

My father went upstairs and in a few minutes they came down together. We sat down to dinner and my mother served the meal she'd been fussing with all day as if it were something she'd whipped up in the last five minutes. She'd made some fantastic Chinese dishes: shrimp rolls and the Chinese pancakes you roll around pork, and a duck concoction with pea pods. My father oohed and aahed and grinned at her like he hadn't lived with her for seventeen years and didn't know she was a terrific cook who had taken a course, and then given one at the community center, in Chinese cooking. I still wished I were a million miles away.

"Tell me what you've been doing. How are things at school?" My father was making conversation with me.

"Eveything's fine. I haven't been doing anything much."

"What happened to that book report you

9

were working on? What kind of a mark did you get?"

A *B+*. I should have gotten an *A;* even my spelling was OK."

"So why didn't you?"

I helped myself to some more rice and duck. "I handed it in late."

"That was silly. Why'd you do that?"

"You know why." I spoke very low.

My father gave me a swift glance. "How should I know why? You had it almost finished when . . ." He hesitated. "When I left," he said, swallowing a long drink of tea.

"That's why it was late." I caught my mother's eye in a pleading, warning look.

I guess she was remembering how I had carried on after he had left. I had cried and cried and said I was never going to see him again. I didn't go to see him all the time he was away. He called me up and he wrote letters to me, but I wouldn't change my mind. One day he was waiting for me when I came out of school. He said I was behaving foolishly, that I was being unfair. I told him maybe that was true, but that I was the way I was and I wasn't going to change. I wouldn't even go and have a soda with him. He had helped me with that book report, and it was a week before I could bear to look at it again. That's why it was late. I told Mr. Kendall, my teacher, that my father had been sick and I was too upset to work on it. That's why I'd gotten a *B+* instead of a worse mark.

But my mother didn't have to worry. I wasn't going to tell him all that; I wasn't that stupid or mean.

"Who's your latest boyfriend?" my dad asked.

"I haven't got one."

My dad grinned. "I don't believe it. There must be someone you're giving a hard time. Who's the lucky fellow?"

"I have a date with Bill Sansone Saturday night. But it's our first real date so I don't know if he'll be my boyfriend or not. I haven't made up my mind."

"What's a real date?" my father asked.

"Going out alone. We've been together with other kids."

"Are you always the one who decides?"

"Certainly. Love them and leave them, that's my motto." I was laughing for the first time that evening. "Not like my friend Anabel. She'd cry her eyes out if her boyfriend didn't call her. Not me, I'd just tell him to get lost."

My father frowned. "That doesn't sound like you."

"I've gotten wise," I said.

"Neat, if you can get away with it." My father was looking quizzical. "But what if you really like him and you don't want him to get lost?"

"I'll never cry over any boy. Not me. No boy's worth it."

"Boys aren't all alike," he said, his face serious now. "You can't bunch them all together. Do you feel that way about your girl friends, too?"

"No, of course not. *They're* friends. Boys are different; I don't think of them as friends, like my girl friends. It's all different." The conversation was getting on my nerves.

"Can I be excused?" I asked my mother.

"Don't you want any ice cream?"

"I'll have mine later."

I stood up and went up to my room. I figured they should be alone anyway. My father was a great one to talk about a boy being a friend. What kind of a friend was he? I thought about Bill and went over to my mirror to see if the little pimple I had on my chin was still there. It was. I hoped it would disappear by Saturday night.

Just thinking about Bill made me feel fluttery, although I wouldn't admit it to anyone, even Anabel. Having Bill Sansone ask you for a date was supposed to be something sensational, but no boy was doing me a favor. Not that I was so fantastically popular—Bill was—but I didn't feel a boy was doing me any honor by asking me out. And I really believed that, yet, when Bill had come over to me in the

12

cafeteria and taken my tray to carry it to a table, my heart had started to jump. I could feel my face flush, and I was glad he had the tray or I would have dropped it. I had been furious with myself for being so gross, and in my room thinking about it, I had to laugh at my father for imagining I could think of Bill as a friend, like a girl friend. My father didn't know *anything*. Boys weren't *friends*. I could never in a million years talk to Bill the way I did to Anabel, or feel comfortable with him in the same way. I wouldn't care if Anabel saw me with pimples all over my face—as a matter of fact she had seen me when I was a mess with chicken pox—but I'd been worrying all week that one darned pimple wouldn't disappear by Saturday.

Having my father home was going to make things different. When Mom and I were alone we ate differently, often just a salad and a sandwich instead of a regular dinner, and we ate at odd times. Sometimes we got into our bathrobes and ate in front of the TV. A few times Mom said it was different when there wasn't a man in the house, and, believe me, it was. She hadn't been at her best these past few months, naturally, but in some ways she had been more relaxed. She had talked more to me, and I had the feeling that although she said she loved him—I don't know how she could after what he did—it was a relief to her not to have to worry about his moods, or his yelling at me, or whether she remembered to get the car serviced. She knew it was different being with a man even if he was her husband. You can fall in love with a boy, but have him for a friend— never. I wouldn't trust him.

Chapter Two

THE NEXT DAY AT SCHOOL, THE FIRST THING Anabel asked was, "What happened last night? Did your father come home?" My father's "affair" was one of her favorite topics of conversation. She was my best friend, but sometimes I felt uncomfortable with her deep interest—as if she were watching a serial on TV and couldn't wait to hear the next episode. I didn't find the situation so entertaining.

"Yes, he came home. Nothing happened, at least not that I know of. My mother made a fantastic dinner."

"I suppose they were all lovey-dovey. Do you think he still thinks about Mrs. Craig? Do you think he'll ever see her again?"

"How should I know? He'd better not see her again. I'm always afraid I'm going to bump into her in the village or someplace. I wish she'd move away."

"I should think she would." Anabel left me to go to her math class, and I went to the library to look up a history assignment. I wished she hadn't mentioned Mrs. Craig; I didn't want to think about her. I didn't think about her for long because Bill came along and sat down next to me.

I like Bill, I like him a lot, but he makes me self-conscious most of the time. I don't want to try to impress him the way the other girls do—they really make a fuss about him—so I don't know quite how to act. It's not easy to just act natural with a boy you like, the way you do with anyone else, especially if you really believe no boy is worth worrying about.

"Do you mind scary movies?" Bill asked me.

"I don't like a lot of blood. Why?"

"There's a good movie at the Trans-Lux, but it's supposed to be scary. I thought we could go to it Saturday night."

"I'll take a chance. I can always close my eyes."

"Or hang on to me." He grinned.

I glanced up at him from my history book. Bill's not the best-looking boy around, not like Steve Bernstein. He has a crooked nose—he broke it when he was a little kid—and he's kind of skinny for his height, but he has deep-set dark eyes that look right at you as if he knows what you're thinking. That's one of the things that makes me uncomfortable because I sure don't always want him to know what I'm thinking.

"I'll manage," I told him.

I was kind of dreading Saturday because both my parents would be home. So far things had gone pretty much back to normal: my father coming home tired from work, my mother rushing out to photograph someone or something—she took pictures for a couple of local newspapers—and me usually cooking dinner which we didn't eat until around seven-thirty. Everyone was so busy there wasn't time to know how anyone was *feeling*. On the surface everything seemed smooth, as if nothing had happened, but I was afraid I'd hit my head on a rock if I went below.

Saturday morning my father was going to the dump and then to the nursery to get lime and fertilizer for the lawn, and he asked me to go with him. I didn't feel like going, but I thought I'd better. We hadn't said much to each other since he'd come home, but I was beginning to think that since he *was* home, I'd better accept it. We used to have a good time together, and I missed the discussions we'd had, although I knew I could never feel the same way about him again.

"Come on, Mellie." He opened the car door for me. He looked at my bare legs, and I expected him to tell me to wear socks. It was April and still cool. In Massachusetts it doesn't get hot until real summer. "You're getting brown already," my father said. "How's your tennis? Want to hit some balls this afternoon?"

"I can't. I'm going bike-riding with Anabel. And I have to wash my hair for tonight; it takes forever to dry."

"You're a busy kid. Who are you going out with tonight? You told me, but I forget."

"Bill Sansone. I don't think you know him."

"You like him?"

"Of course, or I wouldn't go out with him."

"What's he like? Why do you like him?"

I glanced at him sideways, but his face didn't show anything. "That's a funny question. Why do you like anyone? Why did you like Mrs. Craig?"

My father scowled. He screws up his face when he doesn't like something, as if it is actually giving him a physical pain.

"I think it would be a very good idea for everyone in this family if you forgot about Mrs. Craig. She happens to be a very nice woman, and whatever happened is in the past. Maybe when you're older you'll understand."

"I'll never understand." Fortunately we arrived at the dump, which ended our conversation. I helped Dad take our garbage out of the back of the station wagon, and then looked around to see what I could find. I have a

18

fantastic old chair in my room that I found there a couple of years ago; my father fixed it, and I painted it a dark Chinese red. I love it. But there wasn't much that day; the only thing I found was a basket I could put a plant in and hang in my room. Things were still sticky between my father and me. I wondered if that would ever change.

Bill arrived wearing plaid slacks and a red-and white-striped shirt. I had on a purple skirt, a magenta pullover, and pale gray tights. Mom said we looked as if we belonged in a Broadway musical comedy, but I thought we looked sharp. We both like clothes; maybe that's why we like each other. Sometimes Bill does weird things. Last winter his Labrador had puppies, but she got sick and couldn't nurse them. Bill brought the four teeny pups to school in a box. Then he got the janitor to let him put them down in the basement. He went down every couple of hours and fed them out of a bottle. He did that for a whole week until the mother could feed them again. I thought it was pretty decent of him.

"We're going to the late movie," he announced when we got into his mother's VW. "That's the only time to see a scary movie."

"What are we going to do until then?"

He looked mysterious. "You'll see."

"Aren't you going to tell me?"

"Don't you like surprises?"

"Only if I know what they are," I said, and we both laughed.

Bill headed the car toward Boston—we lived just outside the city—and in the city he went down some scruffy back streets. "Hey, where are you taking me?" I was intrigued but a little nervous.

"To the gypsies," he said, and he turned to me with a grin.

"Gypsies?" I shrieked. "Where?"

"You'll see."

Finally he parked the car on a dark street, and we got out. I held on to his arm as we walked past some dilapidated, old houses, until we came to a brownstone that was a little neater than the rest. Stuck in a downstairs front window was a small sign that said MA-DAME ESMERALDA.

Bill started to go up the front steps. "I don't want to go in there," I said, holding back.

"It's OK. Don't you want your fortune told? She reads palms and uses cards. My mother and some friends came to see her, and I heard my mother say she was fabulous. I thought it would be fun."

"Does your mother know we're going?"

"Of course not. It's all right for her, but she'd say I was wasting my money."

"Is it very expensive?"

20

"Nothing's too expensive for you," he said with an elaborate flourish.

"That's nice. I saw a beautiful Ferrari the other day. . . " We both giggled.

The inside of the house didn't seem as though anything going on in it would be very expensive. Mixed in with the musty smell of incense was the strong odor of food cooking, and the hall was so dark that at first I couldn't see. When my eyes became accustomed to the dim light I made out an old-fashioned coat stand, a small table with a bowl of droopy artificial flowers on it, and a beaded curtain that led into another room.

I clutched Bill when a tall, dark woman with long black hair stepped out from behind the curtain. She wasn't fat, but covered as she was from her throat to her feet in a full dark robe that by contrast made her teeth shine very white and her eyes glisten, she seemed huge. She scared the wits out of me.

When she spoke her voice was very soft. "How do you do? Have you come to have your fortunes told?" Her sharp eyes looked us over thoroughly. I had the feeling she was trying to decide if we had any money. "You can have a five-dollar reading or a ten-dollar reading," she said.

I nudged Bill before he could answer.

"Five dollars." I hissed.

She ignored me and kept looking at Bill, but

21

he nodded his head and said the five-dollar one would be fine.

She motioned us to follow her into the room beyond the curtain. The smell of incense was much stronger in the small, stuffy room. The windows were covered with a heavy brocaded material, and I felt as if I were in a closet.

"I'll take you first," she said, motioning me to sit down on a straight chair that faced hers across a table. She indicated that Bill should pull up a chair alongside. My heart was beating fast as she dealt out Taro cards and studied them somberly. She shook her head gloomily and I thought, Oh my God, is she going to tell me I'm going to die of some horrible disease?

"I see trouble." She spoke with a slight accent. "Trouble with a man . . ." She closed her eyes for a moment. "An older man," she said. "Maybe a teacher, no, someone in your family. Your father? Is he ill? Maybe he is sick, maybe some other kind of trouble. You worry about it. You are not very happy, you like everything to be just so, and now it is not." She moved her hand. "You are like this, up and down. Sometimes you are very angry. You want to be the boss, in control; you do not like for someone to take advantage of you. You do not trust people easily. You are going to have an unhappy experience with a male, a boy perhaps, and later you will feel sorry. You are going to lose something, and also you will have

22

a surprise. Soon you will go on a short trip; I see you with people around you. You worry that people are going to hurt you, so you act as if you do not care, but you do. You get hurt easily and that makes for much unhappiness. But there is a strong lifeline for you in the cards, you will live a long time and have many experiences, some sad but on the whole mostly good." She picked up my hand, palm up, and studied it. "Yes, a good lifeline. I am relieved; for someone young I do not like to see a broken line."

She told me a few more things—about how I should work hard at what I do and not worry so much about anyone taking advantage of me—and then she said she was ready for Bill.

I was so busy thinking about what she had told me, I didn't listen too carefully to Bill's reading. She did say that he was very sure of himself, that he should not lose his confidence when things went against him, and she also mentioned some stuff about a trip and getting news in the mail.

"What do you think?" I asked Bill when we left. "You believe anything she said?"

"Who knows? I believe some of it. Are the things she said about you true?"

"I certainly don't like to have anyone take advantage of me, I know that. I don't think I want to be in control, do you?"

Bill laughed. "Of course you do. Most girls

do. The stuff about their being the weaker sex is rot; women are strong. My mother is, I'll bet your mother is, too. My mom can get anything out of my dad that she wants."

"I don't think that's true of my mother. I think my father takes advantage of her."

"I doubt it. I'll bet she does exactly what she wants to do."

We got to the movie just as the picture was starting, and right from the beginning it was scary—one of those movies where a maniac is stalking a young girl, and every time he appears on the screen the audience yells. I grabbed hold of Bill. When he held me close I wished the picture would never end and I could just sit that way in the dark with his arms around me. But at the end of the movie, the evening wasn't over because Bill suggested we stop for a pizza, and I was glad he did.

There were quite a few kids from school at the pizza place, but Bill led me, holding my hand, past everyone to a booth in the back where he said it would be quiet and we could talk. He made me feel special as if I were someone important to him. He ordered a pizza for the two of us and sat back and looked at me as if he were concentrating on remembering every feature of my face. But his eyes were soft and I thought, he's different from other boys. He makes me feel soft, as if I want to open my arms to the world, to embrace everyone because the world is beautiful and good. It sounds mushy and awful, but Bill made me feel mushy and good.

"We're going to have a wonderful summer," he said as if that was all decided. School was going to be over in about six weeks, so it was almost summer. "Do you like going to the flea market? There's a great big one every Saturday; I love it. You can find really neat things. I got some super stones there. Maybe I'll make some jewelry someday. And old bottles, wait till you see my collection of old bottles."

"Sounds like fun. I pick things up at the dump, but I haven't been to the flea market. I'd love to go."

"And I think I'm getting a canoe. It's not a new one, but a friend of my father's wants to sell one. Maybe my parents will give it to me for my birthday. We can take it on the river and have picnics. Just the two of us. I don't like going out with a crowd, do you?"

"Not all the time," I said cautiously. "Parties are fun sometimes."

"Sure, I didn't mean that. I'm not a hermit. But if two people really like each other, it's nice to be alone. I like to really get to know someone. Maybe someday I'll be a psychiatrist, or a writer. I like to know all about people, what they think and what makes them do what they do."

"I think about that a lot." I was thinking of

25

my father; what made him do what he did? And my mother, too, what went on in her head having him home now? I was tempted to tell Bill about them, but I decided against it. I guess I'd rather have other people tell me about themselves than tell them about me. I liked the way Bill ate his pizza, real neat, not letting it drip all over him the way most boys do.

When we left he drove around for a while. I was both nervous and excited wondering if he was going to park. Of course he did. I felt very close to him when he kissed me, as if I understood what it meant when someone "melted with love." Sitting in the dark in his car we could have been in another world, or on a South sea island, removed from everyone. I'm in love, I thought, really and truly in love. Every time he touched me I had the same melting feeling, and when I looked into his face and saw his desire and yearning I knew it was love. Yet I felt I could trust him, as if all my tough talk about never trusting anyone was being wiped away.

"You're beautiful," Bill whispered. "I love you."

When he got too passionate and I let him know he had to stop, he kissed me gently and we both sat back. We hardly spoke, but he held my hand tightly until he drove me home.

Chapter Three

THE NEXT MORNING, SUNDAY, WHEN I WOKE up the first thing I thought was that I had made a terrible fool of myself the night before. I was as bad as, worse than, all the other girls who played up to Bill's ego, who let him think he was irresistible. I had done the same, and more. I had *believed* him when he had kissed me so passionately, when he said that he loved me. I had felt so trusting, so ready to love him back.

What a stupid fool I was. I, of all people, who knew better. I could barely look at myself in the mirror—at the face that stared back at me, at my big dark eyes and wide mouth. For a few moments I looked at my mouth and I could almost feel the crush of Bill's face against mine, and then I wiped my hand across my mouth as if to remove the last memory of his touch. I scrubbed my face with soap and water.

My parents were in the kitchen when I came downstairs. My mother was standing at the counter making orange juice, and when I walked in my father was in back of her with his arms around her waist. I felt oddly embarrassed as if I had surprised them at something, although certainly I had seen my father hugging my mother hundreds of times before. But everything was different now. I thought immediately, had he stood that way with Mrs. Craig? And then I thought of Bill. How many girls had he kissed the way he had kissed me? How could you believe anyone?

My father turned from my mother and kissed me good morning on my forehead. "Did you have a good time last night? How was your date?"

"It was OK."

"Just OK? That doesn't sound so good. Anything wrong?"

"No, I said it was OK."

"All right, all right. You sound pretty grumpy."

"Maybe I feel grumpy."

"Melissa's been having rather a hard time," my mother said soothingly. "She's going through a stage. At fifteen you have a lot of feelings you don't know what to do with."

"Nonsense," my father said. "That kid's got

everything, but she's been moping around this house ever since I came home." He spun around and put his hands on my arms. "Aren't you glad I'm home? Aren't you glad you've got both your parents instead of being another kid with divorced ones? Would you like to be shuttled back and forth from one parent to another like a Ping-Pong ball?"

"Leave me alone. Please leave me alone." I was fighting back my tears.

My father dropped his arms. "I'm sorry," he said morosely. He looked at me like a whipped dog. "I thought you'd be happy that your mother and I were together. Oh, God, am I to be punished forever because I made a mistake?"

I ran out of the kitchen and up to my room. I got back into bed and put the covers over my head. I might have stayed there all day if it hadn't been for Anabel. In a little while she called up, and my father insisted that I come down to talk to her. She said that I sounded awful and that she'd pick me up at noon. She said there was going to be a soccer game at one o'clock and we should go and watch it. I didn't want to stay home so I said OK.

Then I started worrying about whether Bill was going to call. I wanted him to desperately, but I felt nervous—afraid that if he did, I wouldn't know what to say to him. My mom was right. I had so many mixed feelings, I

29

didn't know what to do with them. Why should I want him to call when I didn't believe him, and why should I change my blouse three times before I picked the right one to be wearing in case he'd be at the soccer game?

My parents looked droopy when I came back downstairs. Oh Lord, I thought, I hope they haven't been fighting. It was as though we were all three watching each other every minute. I thought of hostages with a guard over them: each time one person made a move the rest were looking to see what he or she was doing. I told them I was going out with Anabel and they both look relieved.

"How was your date with Bill? Anabel asked the minute we met. As we started to walk to the ball field, I told her about the fortune teller and the movie and the pizza but not about our parking. "Do you like him?" she asked.

"He's OK. What about you and Peter? What did you do?" Peter Nickerson was her boyfriend.

"Nothing much. My parents went out so we just stayed home and played records." Anabel wasn't looking at me and her face was flushed.

"You did more than play records," I said, with a giggle.

Then she looked at me. "Peter and I really care about each other. We've been going together for over a year. He's sixteen now and I'm almost sixteen. We don't do anything wrong."

"How do you know he really cares about you? In school he seems pretty friendly with Dodie Marks. Doesn't that bother you?"

"He and Dodie are old friends, their parents are friends. He's not in love with her. My Cousin George and I are good friends, so what?"

"George is your cousin; that's different. You're pretty naive, trusting Peter the way you do. I wouldn't."

"You and I are different," Anabel said. Her delicate, small face looked worried though. Anabel was one of those girls who could look absolutely beautiful one day and washed out the next. She was petite, with a tiny waist and small bones, and the most gorgeous long blond hair. She looked very pretty that day and standing next to her with my long legs and strong somewhat flat body, she made me feel big and athletic. I didn't have her soft curves, but I did have a good flat belly and bumps in the right places.

"Don't worry about it," I said. "I'm sure Peter's mad about you." I wanted to reassure her although I didn't believe any boy was to be trusted.

Soon after we got to the ball field, Bill came

along. He came right over to us. "I thought I'd find you here," he said, then added to me, "I called your house. Your father said you were meeting Anabel so I figured you'd be here."

The three of us climbed up onto the benches and sat down, with me in the middle between Anabel and Bill. It was a good game although not terribly exciting because it was between two of our own high-school teams. But we did a lot of jumping up and down. Bill had hold of my hand, and I felt close to him again. Out there in the bright sunshine, with Anabel on one side and Bill squeezing my hand on the other, it seemed as if the world was a good place, and my fears of the morning fell away.

But not for long. Marie Dupré came along. Bill waved to her, so she climbed up and sat down on the other side of him. Marie was a French exchange student, and with her cute French accent and mispronounced English words, she'd made rather a hit in school. She had an interesting intense face and was supposed to be terribly smart. Bill, a senior, was in his fourth year of French, so the two of them began yakking in French like crazy. The brightness of the day faded for me.

It was no comfort that Bill held on to my hand while he was talking and laughing so happily with Marie; that is, he did until I drew it away. It wasn't that I was jealous of Marie. I hardly knew her, but from everything I'd heard she was OK, real studious. It was Bill. He was throwing back his head, laughing uproariously at his own mistakes in French, and having such a good time, I could just see him holding her and kissing her the same way he had me. I had been right. I'd been a dumb fool to have thought otherwise, to have believed what he'd said and to have fallen for all that passionate stuff the night before.

I thought about my mother. She had believed my dad and look what had happened to her. I wasn't going to be that foolish. They say that they love you and that you are beautiful, blah, blah, just to get what they want. Like my father saying so sincerely—(ha-ha)—that he loved my mother, then going off to be with Mrs. Craig for three months. How dumb do they think we are? I decided to play it cool.

After the game, Anabel said that Peter was coming to her house, and she invited us all to do the same. Bill looked at me and said, "OK?"

"Sure, why not?"

Marie said she had to go home, but I heard Bill remind her they were to meet in the library on Monday. "Remember, you promised to help me with that translation," he said.

"I remember; do not worry. I'll be there."

"She's a good kid," Bill said. "I feel sorry

for her, so far from home. Sometimes she gets terribly homesick she told me."

"Well, she has you to help her," I said.

"Yeah, I do what I can. But she helps me more than I do her. She's been terrific helping me with my French."

"I'll bet."

Bill looked at me and then laughed. "We're just friends, Melissa." We'd been walking slightly behind Anabel, and Bill picked up my hand and held it.

It was a funny evening. Anabel said her parents weren't coming home until later, so we could stay and make spaghetti for supper. I called home, and my mother said it was OK. When Peter came over, the four of us sat around and talked and played records. Anabel wanted to watch "Love Boat" so we did that. But Bill kept looking at me as if he was trying to decide something or figure something out, although he was acting all the time as if I was his girl. He talked some more about all the things he wanted to do over the summer and spoke as though he was including me in most of them. I just kept quiet.

We ate in Anabel's TV room, and I sat down on a chair next to a little table with my plate of spaghetti. "Come on over here," Bill said. He was on a big cushion on the floor, and he pulled another one over close to him.

"I'm comfortable here."

34

"Then I'll come over to you," he said with a grin. He pulled his cushion over as close as he could and he sat so he could share my table. He was so nice to me all evening, bringing me dessert and asking if I wanted more, and never stopping looking at me. I felt myself melting.

"Bill's crazy about you," Anabel said when we were in the kitchen alone for a few minutes. I just shrugged.

It was late when he walked me home. My parents were in bed already, and Bill came into the sun parlor in the back of our house. Without a word he took me in his arms and kissed me just the way he had the night before. At first I pulled away, but he looked so hurt and bewildered. Then with an intense, concerned expression, he said, "What is the matter?" I couldn't say anything. We kissed and held each other the way we had before, and I thought, this is real; this is it. We *are* in love.

"You acted so peculiar all evening, I was afraid," Bill said.

"Afraid of what?"

"Afraid you didn't like me anymore. Don't do that, promise?"

"I'll try," I said.

Suddenly going to school became exciting because I knew I would see Bill. My mother couldn't get over how fussy I was about my clothes, ironing my blouses and even some-times pressing my jeans. Bill went in for crazy clothes, but he noticed those things. We almost always had lunch together, and in the after-noons if he had ball practice, I'd go and watch him, or if not, we'd go for a walk or a bike ride. Every once in a while I worried when I saw him talking to Marie Dupré, or when he was doing some research with her in the library, but I tried to put suspicious thoughts out of my mind.

I felt so good I almost forgave my father.

I had to do a social-study paper on the reconstruction period in the South, and my father told me to read Bruce Catton for back-ground material on the Civil War. He also gave me a list of other books to read. "I can't read all those," I told him.

"They're interesting; you'll like them even if you don't have to read them for school." I did get interested, and my father and I discussed them in the evening. It was almost like old times.

My father and I had long talks about the problems in the South after the war. Freedom, he said, had been an empty word for many blacks who had been completely dependent on the white families they worked for. They had no education, no way to make a living, no-where to go. My dad knew so much about it that he was able to show me the connection between the past and the civil-rights movement today.

But about two weeks after I'd fallen in love with Bill—I was feeling good—the bubble burst. The first thing that happened was a fight between my mother and father. I could hear them from my room where I was trying to do my homework. I always left my door open a little because for some reason I felt safer that way.

They had probably begun by talking quietly, but I became aware of their argument when I heard my father yelling. "It's business, I can't help it. It's not my fault she took a job with an environmental agency. What do you want me to do, quit my job? You're being very silly. I'm not meeting her anyplace. Marilyn is coming to my office; my secretary will be there, the whole blasted office will be there."

"You promised that you would never see that woman again. She could see someone else; she doesn't have to see you. I'll bet she took that job just so she'd *have* a reason to see you." My mother's voice broke into a sob.

"Oh, God, I never should have told you. I was dumb enough to think this would prove to you once and for all, that it is over. That seeing her doesn't mean a thing to me. I wanted you to stop thinking about it."

37

"I'll never stop thinking about it if you're seeing her," my mother said, sobbing. "If she was any kind of a decent person she'd move away; she'd let us live in peace."

"Darling,"—my father's voice was softer—"I can't control what she does. Maybe she can't move; I don't know. Her parents aren't far away and her mother's not well. . . . There may be a lot of reasons why she's living here. But that has nothing to do with us, with you and me. . . ."

"But it does. Now you're defending her. How can I believe you're not still interested?"

"Because I'm here." My father was yelling again. "Because I love you. If I loved her I would have stayed with her. Why do you think I wanted so terribly to come home? I wanted to be with you and Melissa. You're my family; you belong to me and I belong to you. It didn't take me long to find that out."

"Three months . . ." my mother said, and then she ran up to her room sobbing, and I heard my father slam out of the house and get into his car. His tires screeched as he skidded out of the driveway.

I put my history book down. I had read one paragraph over four times and I still didn't know a word in it. Should I go in to see my mother? I didn't know. She had closed her door. I was very frightened. Where had my father gone? Had he gone back to Marilyn Craig? Was it all going to start all over again?

I kept going to the window to see if my father was coming home. After a while my mother came out of her room, and seeing my door open, she came in and sat down on my bed. She looked awful. Her eyes were red and swollen and her whole body looked dejected. "I suppose you heard your father and me." She looked at me with large, anxious eyes.

I nodded. "I couldn't help it."

She gave me a weak smile. "I'm not blaming you. The whole street may have heard us; we were yelling so loud." She almost started to cry again, but she controlled herself. "I don't want you to worry about it. Everything's going to be all right. We had fights before all this happened; it's nothing new. Married people have disagreements."

"This is rather different, though, isn't it? Is he really going to see that woman?"

"She has to come up to his office on some business. He said it was better than meeting her somewhere else, and I suppose he's right. Trusting is part of loving, Mellie."

"But you can't just trust blindly. Mom, don't let him hurt you again. We can get along without him, you and me."

The tears welled up in Mom's eyes. She took me in her arms and hugged me. "I love him,

Mellie. I don't want to lose him. I don't want to chase him away."

We hugged each other, but I didn't say anything. I didn't know what I wished, whether I wanted him to come home or not.

I guess he came home late, after I was asleep, because the next morning he was there, in the kitchen scrambling eggs. My mother was a little too cheerful and my father a little too solicitous and subdued. Obviously they had made up. My mother never ate eggs in the morning, but my father dished out a plate for her and she ate them. People are crazy, I thought, and if this is what love is all about, I can live without it.

But, of course, when I saw Bill in school later, I decided that we were different. I had such a fierce yearning for him it was a good thing we were in school and not alone, or I don't know what would have happened. He looked so fresh and clean, and when he stopped me in the hall and held my hand for a minute, his eyes were so tender I wanted to die.

"Don't forget the flea market's on Saturday. I'll pick you up around noon. They have a food stand where we can get hot dogs, OK?"

"Sure, great. I think I'll bring ten dollars, and that'll be all I can spend."

"Me, too, unless my mother gives me more. I'd like to find some old posters or pictures for my room. Sometimes they have some real crazy old pictures, nymphs sitting by a waterfall, stuff like that."

"You mean naked girls. Just what you need."

"No picture can excite me as much as you," Bill whispered.

Chapter Four

THE SUN WOKE ME UP ON SATURDAY MORNing, but I didn't mind because I was so glad it was going to be a good day. I lay in bed for a while thinking about the hours to come—a whole day with Bill. It was going to be wonderful, from noon on. After the flea market we were going to bring his mother's car back—his father was home on Saturday which was why he could get his mother's car—and then we were going over to Anabel's for a cookout. We had been planning it all week.

I'd decided days ago what I was going to wear. A new bright turquoise cotton skirt and a plain navy scoop-neck top. I was beginning to get some tan, and the outfit really looked good. I had just come out of the shower when Mom called from downstairs to say Bill was on the phone. "Do you want to call him back?"

"No, I'll come down." I tied on my robe and went to the phone.

"Melissa, I have bad news," Bill said.

"What happened? Are you all right?" My heart was skipping nervously.

"I'm fine. No, it's that my grandparents are coming. My mother said I knew about it, but I swear I didn't. Anyway I've got to stay home. Some aunts and uncles and cousins are coming over, too; it's a family party. I had a fight with my mother, but she said I can see you anytime, and the flea market'll be there next week. Anyway she won't give me the car, so there's no way we could go. I feel rotten, but we can go next Saturday.

There was a dead silence. I was too stunned to speak.

"Hey, are you there? I'm sorry, honestly, I feel terrible."

"I'll bet you do."

"Hey, don't be mad at me. I feel as badly as you do. It's not my fault. Tell Anabel I'm sorry, will you?"

"You can tell Anabel yourself. It doesn't matter. Forget it. Good-bye." I hung up.

I ran back up to my room and closed the door. I couldn't believe it. We had talked about this day so much. If he had really wanted to go, he could have persuaded his mother. At least he could have gone to the flea market and then gone home to see his grandparents. The whole story sounded fishy to me. At first I was too disappointed to feel anything else, but later I started to work myself up into a furious boil.

For Bill to call me up at the last minute like that with such a dumb story— He was certainly taking me for an awful fool. A picture of Marie and Bill popped into my head, and I became convinced he had broken the date with me in order to be with her. Just yesterday I had seen them headed for the library togther, and I felt as certain as if I actually saw him that Bill was headed for Marie's, probably that very minute. Tears streaming down my face, I hung my skirt back in the closet.

"Melissa," my mother was calling. "Dad and I are leaving. Are you coming down?"

"No, go ahead. Have a good time," I said weakly. They were going off to play golf.

"Thanks. You have a good time. When will you be home?"

"I don't know. Not late." I couldn't get myself to tell her what had happened.

"We'll be back around five, but just to change our clothes; then we're going out to dinner with the Osbornes."

I heard the door close and Dad's car come out of the garage. I was alone in the house. I felt ashamed to have been so dumb. I should have known better; I did know better. Who should know better than I not to trust a boy? He kisses you and tells you that he loves you, and then, poof, when he feels like it he just drops you. Why do they use the word love? Love is supposed to mean something deep and lasting. I never want to hear a boy say he loves me. It's an insult to be lied to.

It took me a long time to feel steady enough to call Anabel. I got annoyed when she defended Bill. "Why do you think it's a fishy story?" she asked. "It sounds like his mother. Honestly, Mellie, you're too suspicious."

"I have reason to be," I said. "He would have known if his grandmother was coming."

"Not necessarily. Maybe it was just arranged. Anyway, what are you going to do?"

"Mope, I guess. There's nothing to do."

"You can come over this afternoon; I have to go shopping with my mother this morning. Peter'll be coming over later. We can still have a cookout."

"No, thanks; I don't think so."

"I wish you would."

"No, I'll stay home."

It was easily the worst day in my whole life. Around noon I dialed Bill's number just to see if he was home with his family—I planned to hang up as soon as anyone answered—but there wasn't any answer. Then I was positive he'd given me a made-up story. If they were having a family party, they'd be home, wouldn't they?

When I'm depressed and gloomy I eat a lot,

and I think all I did that day was eat. Fortunately I don't get fat, but that Saturday I should have gained ten pounds. I had two huge bologna sandwiches on rye bread, about a dozen brownies, three bananas, and a pint of vanilla-fudge ice cream. By five o'clock I felt sick, and when my parents came home, I was on my bed. I told them I'd broken the date because I wasn't feeling well. Of course, my mother immediately took my temperature, but I had no fever.

Then my father made the mistake of teasing me and saying that probably I'd had a "love spat" with Bill. That got me mad. "I had no love spat," I yelled at him. "Bill's a creep anyway. I'm not the least bit interested in him."

"I thought you were crazy about him," my mother said. "You talk to him on the phone every night for hours after seeing him in school all day. I'll bet you did have a fight. Maybe you're taking it too seriously."

"You two know nothing about it. What do you know about love anyway? You're the last people to give me advice."

My father looked at me sternly. "I think we know a lot more than you do. And you have a lot to learn about relationships."

"I'll never learn from you." I turned away from them. "I thought you were going out for

46

dinner." I didn't want to discuss anything with them anymore.

"We are," my mother said. "What about you? Do you want me to fix you something before I go? Some hot soup?"

"No, thank you."

I was glad when they left, that is if a person can feel glad about anything when she's depressed beyond words. What made me feel worse was that I knew I couldn't talk about my feelings to my parents. There was a time when I might have, but not now. There was a wall between us. I felt that they were being hypocrites, acting as if everything was all right, that they had a happy marriage, when there had to be Mrs. Craig between them, like a festering sore. I mean, how could my mother forget it? Or my father either?

I was only a kid, but I already knew that there was no such thing as true love. They didn't have to teach me about relationships. I knew that a boy could get me all excited, that I liked him to kiss me and touch me—if he was the kind of boy I liked—but to believe that he really loved me was just plain stupid.

To add to my misery, in school on Monday, I got bawled out by Mr. MacDonald, my language teacher. He called on me to answer a question, and I hadn't even heard it.

47

"Melissa apparently isn't interested in what we are doing," he said sarcastically. "Perhaps you could honor us by reading the next paragraph in the text," he said.

My book wasn't even open, I didn't know what page, what text. I could feel my face flame while I fumbled through the book for a few seconds.

"Never mind," he said coldly. "Susan, you read it. And Melissa, you can stay after class please."

Mr. MacDonald is a thin man with a sallow face and deeply set, piercing eyes. He's very smart, but to get a smile out of him is an accomplishment. "Your written work isn't that good," he said to me after the bell rang, "that you can afford not to pay attention in class."

"Yes, sir."

"Yes, sir; yes, sir. What does that mean? I don't need to be yessed. What do you intend to do about it?"

"Pay attention, sir."

"Perhaps it may help if you write a short essay on the use of the subjunctive case. About five hundred words." He looked at me with something that might pass for a smile.

I swallowed hard. "When do you want it?"

"By the end of the week."

Out in the hall Bill was waiting for me. "Can you come to the library, or do you have a class?" he asked.

"I have a study period, but I'm going to work in the shop." I tried not to look at him. "Where's your girl friend you usually go to the library with?"

"Marie? She's not my girl friend. Listen, I'm really sorry about Saturday. I felt awful all day thinking about what a good time we could have been having. Next Saturday for sure?"

"No next Saturday. You felt so awful, you and your family all went out." I hadn't meant to say it, but it came out.

"What do you mean?"

"I tried calling you, to see if you wanted to go over to Anabel's later," I lied. "Nobody was home."

"We were home all day."

"No one answered the phone."

"Oh, my uncle had a new car so we all went for a ride, just a short ride. You must have called then. What's the matter, don't you believe me?"

"No, I don't believe you. And I don't like dates broken at the last minute, thank you." I walked away.

"Melissa . . ."

I didn't answer. That was that.

In the shop I was making a box for holding wood; I was going to give it to my parents for a present. It was a pretty good size, and I had spent a lot of money for the pine boards, so I was taking my time doing it. I wanted it to be just right. I had the bottom and two sides on, and I was cutting the wood for the back when Jimmy Ferris came in. Jimmy is a blond freckle-faced boy who goes around looking cheerful all the time. I'd known him since fourth grade, but not well, even though occasionally we'd been at the same parties. Jimmy never went with any one crowd; he just floated around. Everyone liked him, although I never heard of anyone being crazy about him. He was someone who was just there.

"Want any help?" Jimmy asked.

"If you wanted to hold this board down for me I wouldn't mind." I had to cut about a foot off to get the right length. When Jimmy held the board, the saw went through it like a knife cutting butter. I held it in place, and it fit exactly.

"It's going to be beautiful, isn't it?" I stood back to admire my work although the board was only stuck in.

"Yeah, it is." Jimmy was looking at me and not at the wood box. "You still going with Bill Sansone?" he asked casually.

"I'm not going with anyone," I said. "Why?"

"Just asking. For a funny-looking little kid you didn't turn out so bad," he said with a grin, still eyeing me up and down. "We've known each other a long time, haven't we?"

"Remember Miss Davies, our fourth-grade teacher? How I hated her. She hit me across the knuckles once with a ruler; it hurt like the devil. That woman was sadistic." I looked him up and down. "You were a cute-looking little boy. You haven't changed that much; you still have that all-American face. I don't know why, but you make me think of the Hardy Boys."

"You read books like that?"

"I used to. My father has them all."

"You're a funny girl. You don't look like someone who'd be reading boys' books and working in shop."

"Why not? You think just because a girl doesn't look boyish she belongs in the kitchen making fudge?" I looked down at the skirt I was wearing. "You don't like skirts on girls?"

"I didn't say that. You look OK."

Jimmy wandered off. He was like that, kind of appearing and disappearing. But I thought about him as I hammered the back of the box into place. I wondered what he was really like, who his friends were, what kind of a boy he was.

However, I didn't spend much time thinking about Jimmy Ferris. I had that essay to worry about, and I still felt angry and humiliated by Bill. That was the last time I was going to believe anything a boy said to me.

* * *

Instead of going home from school, Anabel and I walked to the village. "Bill asked me to find out if you were still mad at him," Anabel said.

"Mad is too strong a word. I'd have to care about him to be mad at him. I'm just not interested in Bill."

"I think you're being silly. He really likes you. A person is innocent until he's proven guilty, and you haven't proven anything about Bill."

"I don't have to. I know how I feel and that's enough. I don't want to talk about Bill and you can tell him to go fly a kite."

We stopped and got ice-cream cones, and then we went to the dime store. Anabel bought some cosmetics and I bought notebooks and pencils. Anabel and I were talking as we were going out, and inadvertently I bumped into a lady wearing a hat and sunglasses. I looked up right into the eyes of Mrs. Craig. "Oh, I'm sorry."

"Hello, Melissa," she said. She was flustered and dropped a package she was carrying. Like a dope I bent down to pick it up, and she did too, and, of course, our heads banged together. Mrs. Craig laughed nervously. "I'm sorry."

We both stood up, and as Mrs. Craig went into the store, I went out to join Anabel who had gone ahead.

"Whew." I took hold of Anabel's arm. "That was bound to happen sometime, that I'd run into her. I wish she'd get out of town."

"Do you think your father ever sees her?"

"I don't know," I said testily. "She looks like a cabbage, doesn't she?"

"You used to think she was pretty."

"Did I? I must have been blind. My mother's much prettier."

Anabel looked at me sideways. "You hate her?"

"Sometimes I think about killing her."

"I thought you said everything was all right."

"Oh, sure it is." But of course I knew it wasn't."

I thought seeing Mrs. Craig was the last straw that day, but it wasn't. I went home with Anabel and stayed so long that I had to run home to be in time for supper. I expected to get bawled out for being late, but I found my mother pacing up and down our family room like a nervous cat.

"What's the matter? Where's Dad?"

"I wish I knew." My mother is pretty; she has fair, delicate skin, and kind of childish blue eyes, but when she's anxious or worried she looks like a faded movie star. Her face gets scrunched up. She looked that way then. "He called and said he'd be a little late, but it's past seven and he usually gets home a little after five. That's more than a little late." She looked at me as if I could reassure her. I knew she was thinking the same thing I was: had that woman gone to his office this afternoon?

I remembered Mrs. Craig's face when she'd said hello to me, and how guilty she had looked. Suddenly I felt sure that she was with my father now, and had probably been on her way to see him when we'd met. I had never in my life seen my mother smoke, but she pulled a crumpled package of cigarettes out of her bag and rather savagely lit up. She looked at me apologetically. "I don't really like them," she said, "but I get so nervous. Melissa, do you think . . . ?"

"He's probably just detained at the office." I was defending him for her sake, hating him while I spoke.

"I wish we could move away from here," my mom said, taking a few puffs and then crushing out the butt. "But your father has such a good job that he likes, and jobs aren't easy to get these days. Municipalities are cutting back on hiring planning firms."

I felt that I was getting into my mom's mind, as if she had opened it up so that I could look inside. She probably thought about Mrs. Craig all the time when my father wasn't with her. If he was late, was he seeing her? Did he call her from the office? Even when Mom was with him, did she wonder if he was thinking of that woman? "Oh, Mom." I put my arms around her. "You never should have taken him back."

She held me for a minute or two and then she pulled away and wiped the wetness from her face. "No, you're wrong. I'm not sorry; we'll work it out. We have to. We care about each other. You mustn't feel sorry for me, Mellie. I'm OK. I worry more about you; it's a tough time for all of us, and you're just the wrong age for all this."

"What's the right age?"

Mom laughed. "Younger or older I guess. But fifteen . . ." She shook her head. "You're getting interested in boys yourself; you're changing from a child into a young woman. I don't want you to get the wrong idea about boys, about men, about your father. He's a very decent man. . . . I know that sounds funny coming from me, but believe me, it's true."

I didn't answer. My father's a punk I thought, and my mother is like a scared kid afraid to face the truth. I felt a hundred years older than both of them. No boy or man was going to make a fool of me again.

I put on my sweat suit and went out running. It was staying light later, and the sky was a pale pink. I didn't know where I was going; I didn't care. I just wanted to run and run. I wished I could run off the edge of the earth. I wasn't paying any attention to streets or houses, but as I turned a corner, I heard my name called. I don't like stopping when I've got a good rhythm going, but I was curious. It was Jimmy Ferris. "Hey, you want company?"

"I don't care."

He had on running pants and he fell in alongside me. We went up to an old reservoir and ran around it; then I headed back toward home, and Jimmy just kept on with me. He didn't say a word; neither did I. When we got to his house, he said, "So long," and went up his porch steps. I kept on. I guess we had run together for about half or three-quarters of an hour, and we hadn't said a word all the time. It was strange but quite nice.

It was getting darker by the time I got home, and except for a light in the hall and in the kitchen, the house was dark. My father's car wasn't there; my mother's car was gone, too. I had an awful feeling that I didn't want to go into the house. But I did.

My mother had left a note on the hall table.

> Got tired of waiting, so I went out. Dinner is in the fridge, help yourself.
>
> Love,
Mom

I went upstairs, took a shower, and got into a robe. The house was terribly still. I couldn't decide whether I was hungry or not, but I took out some cold meat and made myself a sandwich. I sat down at the kitchen table, and just looked at the sandwich. I wasn't hungry. The house wasn't entirely quiet; I could hear little creaks, and I hoped no mice were going to come running out of dark corners.

What would I do if my parents never came home? When the telephone rang, I jumped sky-high. It was my mother wanting to know if my father was home yet. "No, he's not. I'm here alone. Where are you?"

"I'm in a bar," she said. "I may get drunk."

"Don't drive if you do," I told her, feeling more like her mother than ever.

"Don't worry, I'll be OK."

It was dark when my father came home. I was curled up in a big chair watching television. I had a glass of soda in one hand and was nibbling at a sandwich held in the other.

"Where's your mother?" he said, hardly nodding to me. "Her car's gone."

"She's in a bar getting drunk," I told him.

"What are you talking about? Turn that thing down, will you? Melissa, where is your mother?"

He turned down the TV, and his face was scowling.

"I told you. She's in a bar getting drunk. I guess she figured that if you could go chasing around, she could too. I don't know why you bothered to come home."

My father straightened up. For a minute I thought he was going to hit me. He turned off the TV, and he looked so angry I was scared. "I don't want you ever to talk that way again. Not ever. Now tell me, if you can, where your mother is."

"I don't know where she is. She called up to see if you were home yet; then she said she was in a bar, and she'd probably get drunk. That's all I know. She waited for ages for you to come home."

"I was at a meeting and then my car broke down. I had to be towed."

I couldn't help smiling. "Dad, you'll have to think of a better story than that. She won't believe you."

"You mind your own business. Damn it, it's the truth. If you know what's good for you, you'll stay out of this and let your mother and me handle our own affairs. I'm going out to look for her."

"She may be down at Sweeney's Pub," I called after him. "It's the nearest."

I heard the door slam behind him. I had had only one small light on while I'd been watching my show, and after he left I sat in the almost-dark room. I didn't turn the TV back on. Men, grown-ups—boy, I was learning fast. They were worse than kids, and I used to believe that they had some kind of superior standard of behavior. Was that phony! I knew that love wasn't one long grand, smooth experience—I wasn't that dumb—but what was it? I had thought I was in love with Bill. When he'd kissed me and held me I'd felt safe and excited and beautiful, but when that had gone sour, I'd been left feeling betrayed. Was that the way it was, just a series of disappointments?

I was in bed when I heard one car come home and both my parents go upstairs. I was too sleepy to get up; I didn't want to anyway. I put my head under the covers and fell asleep.

Chapter Five

THE NEXT MORNING MY MOTHER'S DOOR WAS closed when I got up. Downstairs I could see that my father had had his breakfast and was gone. I didn't know what to do. I wondered if she was sick, if I should knock on her door, or what? After my breakfast, I went upstairs, and it was still quiet in her room. I was worried since usually my mother was up by seven o'clock and it was after eight.

I stood in front of her door, wondering if I would find something awful on the other side. Finally, nervously I knocked softly. "Is that you, Melissa?" My mother sounded very tired.

"Yes. Can I come in?"

She looked awful. There were rings under her eyes, and her face, usually high in color was pale. "I feel terrible," she said. "I guess I have a hangover." She smiled weakly. "I'm not used to drinking more than one drink."

"Did Daddy find you?"

"Yes, thank goodness. And he drove me home. We left my car there. I'll have to get someone to take me over to get it."

"Is Dad coming home tonight?"

My mother frowned. "Yes, of course. Why do you ask?"

"I just wondered. I thought maybe he was leaving again."

My mother raised herself and leaned on one elbow. "He was at a meeting last night and his car broke down." Her voice was shaky.

"I know, he told me. I didn't think you'd believe him."

Now she sat upright. "Of course I believe him. Your father does not lie to me. I trust him."

"You do?" I was honestly surprised.

"Yes, I do. I couldn't live with him if I didn't. I love him and that's what love is all about."

"Then I don't understand love," I said, my voice more emphatic than I intended.

"No, I'm afraid you don't. I hope someday you will. Give it some thought, darling. You'll have to find out for yourself; my telling you won't mean anything."

"I have to go, I'll be late for school. I hope you feel better." I kissed her good-bye with a sad feeling that she was going to cry when she was left alone. I felt sorry for her because I felt so much wiser than she. She was living in an unreal world.

My mother wasn't the only one who upset me that day. I was working on that darned essay in the library, when Anabel came in. We both had a free period, so we sat together in a corner.

"There's a party for Marie a week from Saturday; she's going back to France when school is over. You going?" Anabel asked.

"I haven't been invited. Who's giving it?"

"The Thorpes—where she's been living. You'll get an invitation. Bill asked me to go with him."

"Bill Sansone? What happened to Peter?"

"Nothing. His cousin, Anne, is visiting. If he comes at all, he'll bring her." She certainly surprised me, but she was perfectly calm.

"Anne's not his real cousin; don't you mind?"

"No, why should I? He didn't invite her; their families are old friends, and she and her parents are coming for the weekend. They've known each other since they were babies. Do you mind my going with Bill?"

"No, of course not. I don't see him any-more." I spoke calmly too, but I did have a twinge of jealousy or annoyance; I'm not sure which. Maybe both.

"Anyway Bill and I are just friends."

I looked at her with a shake of my head. "Do you really believe that?"

"Of course I do. We *are* friends."

"Don't be silly. Bill asked you because he wants you to stop going with Peter and to go with him. You'll see."

"That's crazy. You get wild ideas."

"Either that or he wants to make Marie jealous. He's got some motive that isn't innocent friendship; there's no such thing between a girl and a boy."

"You think every boy is out to take advantage of you? I don't believe that." Anabel's soft face was dismayed.

"You'll find out. Look at Peter, just announcing that he's going to take Anne. For all he knew you'd have had to stay home. I don't call that very nice or friendly."

"Anne's coming wasn't his fault. That was all planned before he even knew Marie was having a party. He felt awful when he heard about the party."

"I'll bet. You're as bad as my mother. She's still defending my father, and I'll bet anything he sneaks out to see that Mrs. Craig." I told her about his coming home late the night before. "My mother really believed his story; I wouldn't in a minute."

Anabel kept looking at me as if she couldn't

decide whether to agree with me or not. "I'm sorry about your father," she said, "but not every man has to be that way."

"I'm not taking any chances," I told her.

The worst part about what my father had done—besides hurting my mother—was that I had lost him. Or he had lost me; I didn't know which it was, and it didn't make any difference. I kept thinking about it all that day. Before he had gone away I would have asked him to help me with my essay. He was smart about things like the subjunctive case; he knew so much. But now I wouldn't dream of going to him. I felt that he didn't care that much about me anymore. After all, he must have loved Marilyn Craig an awful lot to leave Mom and me for her. I felt that his coming home didn't change that. He could still be loving her but have come home because it was more convenient than living in a hotel. We had a pretty decent house, and Mom was a good cook and sent his clothes to the cleaners and took care of his laundry. He had it pretty easy at home.

A lot of men did that I was sure, let their wives take care of them at home and went off and played on the outside. I had terrible thoughts about my father all day. Yet, when he came home from work that evening, he was funny and nice and I couldn't think such horrid things about him.

"I bought a present," he said after he'd put a package down on the kitchen table and taken a beer from the fridge. "We're going to have homemade pasta for supper."

"I cooked a chicken," Mom said.

"That'll keep." He unwrapped his package and proudly showed Mom and me a shining silver-colored pasta maker. It really was fun. Dad mixed up a batch of dough, and the three of us took turns putting it through the rollers. When long, thin strips of spaghetti came out, Dad hung them over the kitchen chairs to dry. The place looked crazy with all that spaghetti hanging everyplace you looked. No one said a word about the night before, and Mom looked flushed and happy.

My invitation to Marie's party had come in the mail, and later that evening, Nicky Loewenthal, of all people, called to ask me to go with him. "I hear you and Bill have broken up," he said, "so I hope you can come with me."

"I'd love to," I told him.

Nicky Loewenthal. I was surprised because he's supposed to be a brain, and I always thought he was a bit of a snob. He kept to himself a lot, and except for being a terrific tennis player, he didn't go in for sports. He said that he hated organized games and that tennis was the only game worth the effort. He was like that, having definite ideas and not caring whether anyone agreed with them or not. I wondered why he had asked me to go to the party with him. I had a feeling he was the kind of person who had a reason for everything he did.

When the pasta was dry enough to cook, Mom made a fantastic clam sauce, and we had supper. Dad talked a lot about what was going on in his office, and I felt myself getting nervous that Mrs. Craig's name would pop up. But it didn't. After supper Dad went into his study to do some work, and I helped Mom clean up the kitchen.

I saw her looking at the pasta machine thoughtfully. "It's neat, isn't it?" she said. "A peace offering," she added with a laugh. "Some women get orchids and I get a spaghetti machine."

"I thought you liked it." I gave her a quick glance.

"I do, really I do. It was dear of him to get it. I only hope it wasn't . . ." She didn't finish the sentence.

I looked at her again. In my mind I finished the sentence for her—that it wasn't a guilt offering. Neither one of us said anything more, but I thought, heck, her trust isn't as great as she says it is. No way is she as happy as she's pretending. My poor, sad, mom.

*   *   *

Everyone seemed to be going to the party for Marie. In school the next day Jimmy Ferris asked me if I wanted to go with him, but I told him I couldn't. "I'm really sorry," I said. I was surprised that he had asked me, and intrigued too. In all the years I'd known Jimmy he had never let on that he liked me—you know, the way a boy likes a girl. His asking me to go with him made me wonder what he had in mind all of a sudden. Maybe he was noticing that I wasn't a funny little kid anymore.

For a boy with such an open face, Jimmy was somewhat of a mystery. I wondered if he had ever kissed a girl. He was always friendly, but he seemed wary, too, as if he never wanted to let on how he really felt. It occurred to me that maybe he was afraid of girls, or perhaps he was like me, afraid of getting hurt. But I dismissed that thought as silly; boys didn't worry about things like that.

The Friday before the party my grandmother was coming up from Philadelphia for the weekend. She's a fantastic person and while Mom and she got along great—she's my father's mother—I could tell Mom was nervous about the visit. "She doesn't know anything about Mrs. Craig, or Dad having been away," Mom told me, "so please be careful what you say."

"Why don't you want her to know?"

"There's no point in upsetting her. Besides it's all over and in the past."

"Sure. I won't say anything, don't worry." I looked at Mom and she could tell I had my doubts about its being in the past.

"I wish you'd stop being suspicious," Mom said testily.

"I'm OK. Don't worry about me."

We were in a small room that was Mom's study and she was rearranging her file of photos. She stopped what she was doing and turned to me with a serious face. "I do worry about you. I'm afraid you're getting some wrong ideas in your head."

"Like what?"

"Like breaking off with that nice boy, Bill, just because he had to break a date. He must have felt terrible."

"*He* felt terrible! How do you think I felt? Why are you taking his side? Against your own daughter?"

"I'm not against you, and I'm not taking any side. You like boys, I can tell you do. You like to go out with them, you want them to like you, but you treat them as if they have no feelings. I can tell by the way you talk. You're such a lovely girl, Melissa, but I hate to see you so full of hostility."

"It's not my fault if I am. You'll have to admit I have good reason."

"No, I don't think you do," she said quietly.

68

"You're taking one incident out of seventeen years of a good marriage. Our relationship is better than ever." I raised my eyebrows.

"Don't look at me that way," Mom said angrily. "There's a lot that you don't know."

"I know enough," I said, and left her.

Darn that Mrs. Craig! We used to get along so great, Mom and Dad and me. Now there seemed to be nothing but tension all the time. I wondered if it would ever end. I hated that woman. Why did she have to pick on my father? You'd think her friendship with my mother would have prevented her from having had anything to do with him. I thought about Anabel and me. I'd die without Anabel. Being an only child, I felt as if Anabel was like a sister to me. We told each other everything; there was no boy in the world who could spoil our friendship for each other. Then Bill Sansone popped into my head. I was disturbed that Anabel was going to the party with him, and I had to figure out why. I would have to talk to Anabel about it; that was the great thing about a really good girl friend, to be able to say what bothered you.

Saturday morning my grandmother took a good look at me and said that she was taking me to the beauty parlor for an expensive haircut. "I know just how you need it done," she said. "You'll look terrific."

"OK, I'm game. If I turn out looking awful you'll have to buy me a wig," I teased. She wore beautiful clothes and always looked elegant so I knew I could trust her.

She marched me to the classiest place in town and sat beside me, telling the hairdresser what to do. "Leave it to me, madam," the barber said condescendingly.

Grandma smiled sweetly and said, "I want you to give her bangs and cut it to just above her shoulders, if you please." He gave her a dirty look.

"We will see after I shampoo her, when her hair is wet."

I came from the shampoo, a towel wrapped around my head, to find my grandmother chatting with Mrs. Craig. I was stunned.

It was exactly the kind of place she would be—very jazzy with a lot of pretty boys swishing around and a few competent-looking women. The customers all had extremely long nails, brightly polished, and most of them were having their hair dyed. "Melissa, you know your mother's friend, Mrs. Craig, don't you?" My grandmother looked pleased at having met someone she knew.

"Yes, I do," I said, avoiding Mrs. Craig's eyes.

"She tells me she's working for an environmental agency," my grandmother said. "You must see my son then, he's in the same field.

Are you doing the same kind of work?" she asked.

"Not exactly, but I do know your son, of course. He is a very important man in his field."

My grandmother beamed. She would come home raving about that charming Mrs. Craig who had had such nice things to say about my father. I was usually proud of my grandmother's social grace, but then I couldn't stand her being so nice to that woman. Poor Grandma, she didn't know why I was fidgeting and biting my lip and looking daggers at her.

When she had finished talking about my father and got on to discussing my hair with Mrs. Craig, I couldn't contain myself any longer. "Grandma, let Mr. John do it his way. Since you're spending all that money for a haircut, let him do it his way."

My grandmother looked hurt. "All right, if that's what you want."

Finally Mrs. Craig was called for her appointment and left us. "What's the matter? Don't you like that woman?" my grandmother asked.

"No, I don't."

"I must say you showed it, which I didn't think was very nice. I think she's charming."

I was aching to tell her why I hated Mrs. Craig, but, of course, I couldn't. The whole thing made me hate her all the more. She had

71

no business putting me in that position, and I had an awful suspicion that she had taken some pleasure in doing so. Sitting there talking about my father just like that. How could anyone be such a hypocrite?

My hair looked great, very black and shiny and chic, but I couldn't get out of that beauty parlor fast enough. It was so artificial, like Mrs. Craig smiling at my grandmother so innocently. When we got home I went out for a walk. I wanted to be alone—to think. I think best when I'm walking or running. I was going to be sixteen soon, which, I guess, is still pretty young, yet I felt that my childhood was a hundred years behind me. It seemed as if there had been another world in which my parents and I had had good times together—no fights, no tensions, no suspicions. Ever since I'd been eleven or twelve I'd been looking forward to being sixteen—a driver's license—but now that I was almost there, I was scared; growing up had so many problems.

I thought about the time when I was about five years old and my mother had gone to the hospital for some minor surgery. My grandmother had come up to stay with me, but I had cried my eyes out because I wasn't allowed in the hospital to see my mother. My father had been terrific. He'd taken me to stand outside her window so she could wave to me, and he'd bought her dozens of red roses and me a little corsage of pink ones. It would never have occurred to me in a million years that he could ever stop loving the two of us.

I walked and walked until I was exhausted, and then I decided I had to see Anabel. I had to talk to her because I didn't want anything to happen to our friendship.

She was surprised to see me. "I thought you were spending the day with your grandmother," she said, taking me up to her room.

"Just this morning. I wanted to talk to you."

"Your hair looks fantastic. I love it."

"Thanks." I sat down on her bed. "I need to level with you. Don't look alarmed; it's not a matter of life and death."

Anabel did look worried. "What have I done now?"

"Nothing really. But— It sounds so silly saying it. I feel like an idiot, but I do feel funny about your coming to Marie's party with Bill. I wish I knew why. It isn't that I care about him; it's just—I don't even know."

She really did look upset. "Do you want me to break the date?"

"No, I don't. That would be terrible to do now; besides I want you to come to the party. I'm not making any sense, am I?"

"Not too much. But maybe you do care about him. I thought it was silly of you to break off with him."

"I didn't like what he did."

"All he did was to break a date. Melissa, you just can't stand any kind of rejection; you want to do the rejecting. Ever since that affair of your father's you've been acting funny. I wish you'd forget about it."

"That's what my mother says. But it keeps popping up." I told her about seeing Mrs. Craig in the beauty parlor. "You can't just forget something like that. My mother isn't forgetting it either. Every time he's late coming home, she gets jumpy. She never used to."

"But what do you want me to do about Bill?"

"Nothing. I just needed to talk to you. I guess I'm worried that you're going to start going with him."

Anabel shook her head vehemently. "You don't have to worry about that; I'm not. But even if I were, it shouldn't bother you. If you don't care about him, it shouldn't matter." She smiled uncertainly. "You don't want him, but you don't want anyone else to have him either. That's not nice."

"You're right. But I'm glad I talked to you. You are my very best friend."

"I'm glad," Anabel said. "You're mine, too."

I was relieved I'd talked to her; yet there were things I couldn't talk about. I couldn't tell Anabel I was ashamed I'd let Bill kiss me and touch me—not that I had done it so much as that I had done it with him when he'd turned out not to have given it the same meaning as I had. If he had felt the same, he never would have broken that date. Anabel wouldn't agree with me, but, right or wrong, that was the way I felt. I suppose you could call me disillusioned, which is a terrible thing to be when you're not even sixteen yet.

I was still upstairs when Nicky Loewenthal came to pick me up on Saturday night. When I came down he and my father were involved in a hot discussion about air pollution, how polluted air from one state drifts across to affect the air of other states.

"A farmer in Connecticut may think he's living in clean air while, in fact, he's breathing in carbon monoxide blown in from New York City," my father was saying.

Nicky was listening intently, and I wasn't surprised that when we left he said my father was a terrific guy. "He's so smart. I'll bet you learn a lot from him," Nicky added.

"Some things. Sometimes more than I want to know." I used to be proud of the way my father could charm people, but now it annoyed me. It made me want to say you should know him the way I do.

I wasn't in the best mood for a party in spite of my new haircut, and I wondered why I had come. I didn't like Marie all that much, and having Bill there didn't add to my joy. He came over and said hello and I said hello to him; that was the beginning and end of our conversation. He paid more attention to Marie than he did to his date, Anabel, and once or twice during the evening I saw him whispering to Marie and looking at her with that intense expression I remembered. Only a few weeks ago he had looked at me that way. I turned away from them quickly, with a feeling that I had accidentally seen people at a window who had forgotten to pull down the blinds. I didn't want to see them.

Nick was a very good dancer and we danced together a lot and we ate a lot. Anabel was disappointed that Peter didn't show up, so she asked Bill to take her home early. I think she was hoping to meet Peter later. Bill came back to the party alone. He stayed close to Marie, but when she laughed at whatever he was saying to her—I could imagine what—he'd glance over toward me, as if to say, "See what you're missing? Other girls think I'm pretty terrific."

I was in a funny mood that night; part of the time I felt restless and bored. It must have been around midnight when I picked up someone's sweater and stepped outside. Mr. and Mrs. Thorpe, who had disappeared earlier in the evening, were an older couple who traveled a lot. That's how Marie came to be staying with them, because they had met her parents in France. They had a small but elegant house, and the back of it was landscaped with a rock garden, a small fountain, and a kind of Japanese footbridge that crossed a tiny stream. I walked onto the bridge and looked up at the trees and the stars above. On the other side of the brook there were thick woods that were mysterious and a little scary. I could hear the music and the kids in the house, and their sounds made me feel lonely. They were all couples. Every girl in there, dancing or whatever, had a boyfriend with whom she was in love. At least she thought she was. I didn't think I would ever fall in love.

I could understand married people finding out that they no longer loved each other, or that they couldn't get along. There were enough kids in school with divorced parents. It was pretty tough on them, but at least they knew where they stood. However, with my parents it was different: everything was uncertain. I kept thinking my father would go off again, either back to Mrs. Craig, or even to someone else, or that my mother would get fed up with worrying about where he was. I couldn't count on either one of them.

"Hello, what're you doing out here by yourself?" I jumped so violently that I might have fallen into the brook.

"Don't sneak up on me that way!" I screamed at Jimmy Ferris.

"I'm sorry. I needed air; that place was getting stuffy. I thought it was you here, and I came to make sure. You OK?"

"Yeah, I'm OK. I guess."

"Want to be alone?"

"No, it's all right." He stood alongside of me on the bridge. "How come you didn't bring a girl?"

"I didn't feel like it."

"Do you have a girl friend?"

His teeth shone white in the darkness when he smiled. "I have a lot of girl friends."

"Sounds like a harem. You in love with all of them?"

"I said friends. I'm not in love with any of them. I don't fall in love so easily. I'm fussy."

"Who isn't?" I said, irritated. Who did he think he was? It occurred to me that for all the years I had known Jimmy, he had never tried to kiss me, or made any kind of a pass. Suddenly that intrigued me. He had said more than once that he liked me, that we were old friends, but he certainly didn't show it. I thought it would be fun to see how much he did like me.

I moved over close to him, so close that our arms touched. "It's so quiet and wild here. If it weren't for the music we could be miles away."

"Or on a desert island listening to the na-

78

tives beat the drums. I went on a survival weekend last summer. We really were in the wilderness; it was fantastic."

"What did you do?"

"We learned how to stay warm, and how to build a fire that was safe, and what wild things we could eat and not eat. I could get along if I ever got lost in the woods—or shipwrecked."

"Wouldn't you rather have a girl with you?"

Jimmy laughed. "Depends on who. A lot of girls would be a drag. Speaking of wilderness, have you ever gone white-water canoeing?"

"I've gone on the river." I thought of Bill and his plans to have a canoe for the summer. That was sure out now. "Why?"

"There's going to be a race in July. Starting up at the bridge and going down to below the picnic place on the river. You want to go in it with me?"

"I don't know if I'm good enough for a race."

"We could practice between now and then. You're a good swimmer, and you're strong. You can do it." He was looking me up and down, but I felt he was only trying to judge how well I'd be able to paddle.

"I was never loved for my muscles," I said teasingly.

"Who said I loved you?" he answered with a grin.

"You rat. OK. If you're game, I'm game."

We shook hands on going into the race, but we continued to keep looking at each other. "Have you ever kissed a girl?" I asked him suddenly, feeling bold and mischievous.

Jimmy grinned. "Yes, I've kissed girls. Why do you ask?" He made a gesture toward the sky and woods. "You think this romantic setting calls for making out?"

I don't know if he saw me flush in the dark. "No, you stinker, I don't think it calls for anything." I turned to walk away but he grabbed me and swung me around toward him. He kissed me hard and long and a little roughly.

"Is that better?" he asked, holding my face between his hands.

"You misunderstood me," I mumbled. He had really taken me by surprise.

"I don't think I did," he said quietly. "Listen, I don't fool around just for the heck of it, and I don't like to be dumped. You may think I'm an oddball, but just making out because there's a moon, doesn't thrill me. If I like someone I have to know it's someone I can count on. You understand what I'm talking about?"

"You're hurting me," I said. His hands were holding me tight. "How do you know if you can ever count on anyone?" I asked him when he'd let go of me.

"I'd know. I just would."

We walked back to the house without saying anything more, but I felt that there was more to Jimmy than I knew. He had shaken me up. It seemed as though he had figured out some of the things with which I was still fumbling. It was a disturbing feeling. I wondered how he could be so sure he'd know when he could trust someone.

In the house Nicky asked me where I'd been. I told him, "Outside, looking at the stars."

"With Jimmy Ferris?"

"Part of the time. He followed me out."

"That's not very nice," Nicky said. "Why didn't you ask me to go out with you?"

"I didn't ask Jimmy either. I went out because I felt like being alone for a little while."

Nicky looked at me as if I were a weirdo. "What's wrong with wanting to be alone?" I asked.

Nicky shook his head. "Nothing I guess. Except it's peculiar at a party."

"Then I'm peculiar," I said.

When Nicky took me home, he wasn't backward about wanting to kiss me. My house was dark and we were parked in our driveway. After a few long kisses I really had to struggle to calm him down. "Don't you like me?" Nicky asked.

"I like you OK. But you know, don't go overboard."

Nicky settled back in his seat although he still had his arm around me. "I like your father. He's a terrific guy."

"I'm glad you think so."

Nick was really surprised. "You don't think so?"

"I don't want to talk about my father."

"I was wondering if you'd ask him if he knew of any summer job for me. Office boy, gofer, anything. I'd give anything to work in an agency like his."

I pulled away from him. "Funny, I was wondering why you'd asked me out. Now I know."

Nick was astonished. "What are you talking about?"

"You heard me. Isn't that what you had in mind—that you wanted a job with my father?"

"That's a rotten thing to say. You think I asked you to Marie's party for that? You don't think much of yourself, do you?" His laugh was sarcastic.

"I think a good deal of myself. If you want a job, you'd better ask my father yourself. I'm going in, good night."

I got out of the car before he had a chance to say anything, and went in the back door and up to my room. But I was shaken. I didn't like myself. I didn't like the way I was behaving; I didn't like the thoughts I had. I had been horrible to Nicky.

Still in my clothes, I threw myself down on my bed, and burst into tears. If anyone had asked me, I couldn't have said why I was crying. I mean there was no specific reason. I felt alone, isolated, and afraid of what was happening to me. I was turning into a person I didn't like, a girl no one else would like either. I kept hearing Nick's sarcastic laugh and his voice: "You don't think much of yourself, do you?"

He was right, in a way. Sometimes I felt wiser than the girls, like those who had been at the party that night, who played up to the boys and believed all the stuff they were told—how pretty they were, or what good dancers—but at other times I'd feel I was the one being silly and left out.

I thought about Jimmy, too. He'd made me feel small, but what made him think he was so wise? What did he know about counting on someone? Still his kiss had been terrific and I wondered what it would be like to be the kind of girl he could count on. It was as if my body and my mind were completely out of tune with each other.

After a while I got undressed and climbed into bed. I had no answers for anything.

Chapter Six

IT WAS GREAT BEING OUT OF SCHOOL. I HAD three lawns to mow, one lady's garden to weed, and her house to clean. That gave me lots of time to go swimming and to practice for the canoe race with Jimmy. We went out on the river almost every day that it didn't rain, and we got to a point where we worked well together. We didn't fool around, but worked hard at making time while keeping an even steady pace.

But I couldn't figure him out. Once or twice we went places together, but he never kissed me in that rough, passionate way again. If he'd had a girl I could understand it, but I knew he didn't. And I knew he liked me; I could tell that. But the way he kept his cool bothered me. While I didn't like a boy to paw me, if he didn't even try to give me a real kiss it made me feel I was unattractive.

84

He even took me to the movies a few times, but it was as if I was going out with my brother if I'd had one. One of those times when we'd stopped for a pizza after the movie we were talking about some of the kids in the class. Jimmy said that he thought Marie was sexy.

"Do you think I'm sexy?" I asked him. The question just came out because it had been on my mind.

Jimmy laughed. "Yes, you're sexy. Very."

"Is that good or bad?" I was laughing, too.

"Depends how you use it. It can be very good or it can be a disaster if there's nothing else that goes with it. Anyway you're asking the wrong guy. I like making out, but unless I really care for a girl it's not that much fun. Not all boys want sex just for the sake of sex. I have to really know a girl and like her."

"You've known me for a long time," I murmured.

"We're just really getting to be friends," he said. Then in his exasperating way, he changed the subject. He started to talk about his grandfather who lived with them and whom he adored. "He's terrific," he said. "He's over eighty years old and he's building a stero for me, cabinet and all. I hope I'm like him when I get old."

When Jimmy talked about his family I got a little jealous. He had two older brothers and the whole family did things together. They went off on camping trips and had family ball games. His mother worked and the boys often cooked dinner. He told me his mother had made him clean his room and make his own bed since he was about eight years old. I thought that maybe his family life was why he was so sure of himself, that gave him so much confidence.

I told him a little about my parents, and he made a funny remark. "Is that why you have a chip on your shoulder?"

"I didn't know I did."

"Sometimes. Other times you're OK."

"Thanks a lot." There were times when we were out on the river, especially when we went out at twilight instead of early in the morning, that I felt like getting close to him. I wanted to get past his casual manner, I wanted him to kiss me again the way he did that once. I wondered how he would be if he really cared about a girl. I wanted to really know him, close. That boy was getting under my skin.

But I was having a good time. I really love the summer, and I liked the work I was doing, liked looking forward to canoeing with Jimmy. We were both getting excited about the race. Things at home seemed to be quiet, and I thought life was going back to normal. But then something weird happened.

Mom had to take pictures for the paper at a country fair over in East Botsford, and she asked me if I wanted to go with her. I had a free day with no work so I said sure.

Since the weather was warm and sunny, Mom opened the sunroof on her car, and it was fun driving over there. Mom doesn't like highways so we went there on the back roads; I was amazed that Mom knew where she was going. At home my mother isn't the most organized lady in the world. She forgets things on the stove; she's always looking for her pocketbook or her sunglasses, and she never can find the ticket for the clothes at the cleaners. I used to wonder how she ever got her work done, until I found out that when it came to work she was fantastic. She never forgets her camera or any of her equipment. In a car she's the same way. She knows exactly what she's doing.

We got to the fair late that morning, and it was already crowded. Mom's assignment was just to wander around and take whatever pictures she found interesting. It wasn't a very big fair, but along the midway there were a lot of different games. We stopped at one, and I took shots at some weird little wooden animals. I won a crazy-looking stuffed creature that was kind of a cross between a zebra and a Walt Disney character.

Then we walked into a tent in which there were a lot of booths with things for sale, and Mom spotted a sign: HOMEMADE BAKED GOODS, JAMS, AND JELLIES.

87

"Let's go over there," she said. "I want to buy some; they always have wonderful things made by the women from the church. I'll take a picture of them, too; they'll like the publicity." We walked toward the booth, stopping to look at other displays along the way. Suddenly we were there and facing us across the counter was Marilyn Craig.

I saw her first and tried to steer Mom away, but it was too late. My heart really jumped when I saw them confronting each other. Mrs. Craig's face flushed, but my mother was superb. "I'm from the *Essex County News*," she said calmly. "If you'll stand out of the way, I'll take a shot of what you have on the shelves."

Mrs. Craig stepped aside, but I could see she was churning. She probably wanted to be in the picture. "I'm the chairperson of our auxiliary committee," she said. "If you want any information I can give it to you."

"I don't think I need any, thank you." My mother looked at her and smiled. "I'm familiar with what you do."

Mrs. Craig's face flamed, and she looked as if she'd like to punch my mom in the jaw. Then she turned to me. "Would you like to try a sample of our cheese?" she said, indicating a plate with crackers and small chunks of a yellow cheese. "We're selling whole Vermont cheeses this year."

My mother answered before I could. "Oh,

yes, I'm starving." She helped herself gener-
ously and handed me a couple of crackers piled
with cheese. I didn't feel like eating anything,
but I did. All I wanted was to get away, but my
mother stayed on. She took some more pictures; I think Mrs. Craig had to be in some of
them. Then she deliberately examined the various kinds of jellies and jams, and picked out
one of these or two of those. Meanwhile Mrs.
Craig was getting more and more confused and
upset. I couldn't believe what I was watching.
Those two women used to talk on the phone a
few times a week and be in and out of each
other's houses. I didn't understand how my
mother could stand there and face her, although it was obvious that she was enjoying
herself. I was proud of my mother, but irritated
and impatient, too. "Come on, let's go," I
whispered to her.

"Let me just make sure there's nothing more
I want," she said. We both watched Mrs. Craig
fumble terribly as she made a package.

"I'm afraid I'm not very good at this," Mrs.
Craig said.

"No, you're not. I wonder what you are
good at." my mother said.

Mrs. Craig's face was still flaming. When she
handed my mother the package, my mother
looked her full in the face. "I suppose it was
inevitable that we should meet," my mother
said.

"I'm sorry that we have," Mrs. Craig said.

The air was sparking from the tension between them. I could feel it.

"I imagine you would be." My mother looked thoughtful. "I believe what bothered me the most was that I honestly thought of you as a good friend. That was pretty stupid of me."

"It had nothing to do with you," Mrs. Craig said sharply, but she looked as if she wanted to cry.

"On the contrary, I think it had a lot to do with me." My mother handed me the package. "Would you mind putting this in the car? We don't want to carry it around with us."

I went back to the car feeling terrible. I didn't know what to think; the whole episode had been so full of tension, so full of feelings that were terrifying. When I got to the car, I turned around to see my mother coming up behind me.

"What's the matter?"

"I couldn't stay there; I just couldn't." She had given me the keys so I unlocked the door. My mother got in the passenger side, in front, and burst into tears.

"Mom . . . Mom . . ." I tried to comfort her. "You were terrific, you seemed so calm, so in control. . ."

"I'm not. I never will be," she sobbed. "I hate that woman, and I can't put all the blame on her. Sometimes I hate your father; he shouldn't have done this to me. Yet even when I hate him, I love him. I sound crazy, don't I?"

"No, you're not crazy. Mom, she doesn't matter. Daddy came home because he cares about you."

My mother looked up at me with her tear-stained face. "You're the one who doesn't believe that. I don't always myself. Maybe I shouldn't have let him come home. I worry about what all of this is doing to you. I want you to know about friendship, that real friends have to trust each other."

I looked at her in bewilderment. "Is there any such thing?"

"Yes, of course; that's the point. I *have* to trust your father; I couldn't live with him if I didn't."

"My father? He's not your friend; he's your husband. I thought you were talking about Mrs. Craig."

"Marilyn betrayed our friendship. I had thought she was my friend; that's the point. Friendship has to be based on trust. Of course, Sam is my friend, he's the best friend I have in the world. That's what I want to think," she added wistfully, wiping her face with a tissue.

"I don't understand at all," I said. "Husbands and wives are different from friends." I looked at my mother hesitantly. I thought, she's my mother, not my friend. . . . I can't talk to her the way I can to Anabel, but I did want to tell her what was on my mind. "I mean, with a boy, because there's sex it's more uncertain and emotional than with a friend. That's the way it would be with husbands and wives. You know, Daddy and you and Mrs. Craig? You're not friends; it's just different."

"Not all friendships include sex," she said. "But sex should be only a part of friendship. I hope you'll feel that way when you are ready for sex."

I knew I couldn't discuss this with her. She wouldn't understand at all that when I was with a boy I liked, I had many feelings that had nothing to do with his being a friend. And if friendship included trust, my mother was crazy to mix that up with sex. I still couldn't see how she could trust my father.

My mother would not go back to the fair. "I've seen all of it that I want, and I have enough pictures. They'll have to do."

The next day when I was out in the canoe with Jimmy, I thought about that conversation. Here I was with Jimmy, paddling almost every day, and yet I could not think of him as a friend. We had never so much as kissed since that party—a few times he'd kissed me in fun when I'd done something particularly bright in the canoe, but those weren't real kisses—yet almost every minute I was aware of sex between us. Jimmy had gotten very attractive since I'd known him. His long legs beneath his shorts, were a deep tan; his hair was bleached by the sun and his tan face made his eyes very blue. And I liked his freckles. Still I was unsure of how he felt about me. If he liked me so much, why didn't he ask me to be his girl?

It was late afternoon when we'd gotten on the water, and after working together for a long while, I was tired. Dusk was approaching, and the river was beautiful in the fading summer light. "Let's pull in for a while," I said, pointing my paddle toward a cove. "We can have a swim over there."

Jimmy headed the canoe toward the small inlet, and soon we had pulled it up on shore and were both in the water. The river was always cold, but the water felt marvelous after our sweaty workout. There was no beach, so we climbed on to some flat rocks and stretched out after our swim. I lay on my back, facing the sky, and I could feel Jimmy's eyes on me. I was suntanned too, and just that morning my mom had said, "You're getting a beautiful figure, Mellie." Jimmy was noticing it. I expected him to say something, and was taken aback when he looked around and said, "I think I've been here before."

I raised myself on one elbow. "You have? When? With your girl friend?"

He laughed. "I told you I haven't a girl

friend. But yes, I was here with a friend. A girl who was visiting my cousin and I took her out to show her the river. We went swimming and I'll bet anything it was here."

"Just as I was thinking what a romantic spot we had discovered. You've probably been here with dozens of girls. You're fickle like everyone else," I said teasingly.

"As a matter of fact I'm not," he said quite seriously. "I have no one to be fickle to. I saw a good movie last night," he said, changing the subject.

"Yeah, what?"

"A spy picture, a thriller." He laughed. "I went with Didi. You know her from school. Every time someone got killed she covered her face. It was pretty bloody and gruesome. Do you want to hear about it?"

"Certainly not." I didn't want to hear about his going out with Didi either.

What am I doing here? I wondered. Here I am knocking myself out to go into a canoe race with him, and he sits here, in a gorgeous spot, telling me about taking another girl to the movies. This boy doesn't really care about me. Suddenly I was furious. Me, of all people, to have let myself in for this when I knew one way or another a girl would always be the one to lose out with a boy. They were all the same.

"Come on, let's go," I said.

"I thought you liked it here. What's the hurry?"

"I have to get home," I said.

He looked at me, puzzled. "Your moods change too fast. One minute you're relaxed and friendly, and the next you look like you're cooking up a storm. I can't figure you out."

"Don't try."

That night the storm that had been brewing at home was the one that broke. We were having supper, Mom and Dad and me, when my father said that he had seen the paper with Mom's pictures of the fair.

"I haven't seen the paper yet. Have you got it?" Mom asked.

"Yes, I have it." His face looked grim. "I was surprised to see you'd taken pictures of Marilyn."

"I did? I certainly didn't mean to. I thought I'd taken out any shots of her. Yeah, she was there, big as life. Leave it to that dumb paper to print just the picture I didn't want them to."

My father gave a half smile. "Don't worry, it's a lousy picture. She called me up and told me you insulted her." He wasn't smiling anymore.

"She called you up? Of all the—" My mother was thunderstruck. "First of all I didn't insult her, although I could have. But what did she want you to do? I hope you hung up on her."

"No, I didn't," my father said wearily. "I told her to calm down and forget it."

"How nice of you," my mother said bitterly. She pushed her plate aside and threw down her napkin. "Excuse me," she said as she got up from the table and left the room. My father looked at me miserably. We heard her go upstairs.

"Damn, damn!" he mumbled, and then, giving me a little pat on the shoulder, he got up and followed her. I toyed with some more food, but I soon pushed my plate away. I sat at the table wondering what was going to happen. Who was going to leave now?

Their door was closed and I couldn't hear anything that was happening upstairs. I looked around the room, at my mother's fresh flowers in the bowl, at the antique soup tureen she had recently bought and treasured. It was all a fake, like a stage set, a pretense at having a nice, happy home. Everything was meaningless. I felt reality slipping away from me. My mother liked candles on the table, and in the flickering candlelight, the furniture seemed to be fading into the air. I felt that I was in a room filled with shapes and images that had no substance.

Maybe they were both going to leave, and I'd be here alone.

But it was my mother who left. She called me upstairs and said she was going down to Atlanta to visit her mother and sister for a few days. "Don't worry," she said, her face tight and strained. "I just need to get away for a bit." She tried to smile. "It's not serious. I'll be back. I called my boss and said I wouldn't be gone more than a week. And don't be angry with your father. He's trying."

My father had gone down to get the car out, and then he'd carried Mom's bag to the car. They drove off together to the airport.

I had a terrible feeling of being abandoned when they left. I was terrified that maybe neither of them was ever coming back.

I made myself a cup of tea and sat in the dining room, watching the candles slowly melt down.

Chapter Seven

I REALLY LIKE MOWING LAWNS. IT'S VERY satisfying to cut the swaths of grass and to see the lawn spread like a green carpet behind you. It's also a good way to think, and the next day I was thinking, as I mowed, that my mother was a fool to have left my father here alone. Wouldn't she be throwing him right into the arms of Mrs. Craig? I couldn't keep an eye on him.

That morning he had said he was looking forward to spending time with me alone. "I hardly see you these days; you're so busy," he had said. "Do you want to go out for dinner tonight?"

"I can't. I'm meeting Jimmy at six o'clock to go canoeing. The race is Saturday."

"You're going to have to eat. What about after your canoeing?"

"I'll be tired and I won't feel like getting dressed up and going out. I'll probably eat something before I meet Jimmy. I don't like big dinners anyway."

My father carefully buttered his toast, and then looked at me with a tired expression.

"Why don't you just say you don't want to go out with me?"

"That's not it. We're practicing for the race."

"OK, OK. How are you fixed for money? You need any?"

"I have four hundred dollars in the bank. I'm rich."

My father laughed. "Keep it in the bank. Here's some spending money." He gave me a ten-dollar bill.

"Gee, thanks." He must have seen the surprise on my face.

"It's not what you think. I'm not trying to buy your affection. You really don't think much of me, do you?"

"I don't know what to think," I said, ducking the question.

"Did it ever occur to you that your behavior has an effect on your mother and me? You kids only think about what people, parents especially, do to you. You never think about what you do to them. And boys, too. You're always taking offense because some boy does something to offend you. Maybe they're reacting to something you have done. Have you ever thought of that?"

We were so far apart; he had no idea of the things I thought about. And I couldn't begin to tell him. I felt sad when I kissed him good-bye. He looked lonely and unhappy and I wished my mother hadn't gone away.

When I finished my lawns I went home and stretched out on our hammock in the back-yard. I wondered when my mother would come home, but I kind of liked being alone. It was peaceful. My dad hadn't come home when I left to meet Jimmy to go on the river.

It was windy, and there was a strong current that day. You really had to pay attention in that river because of the rocks. By this time we knew where most of them were, but you could only see the tips of some of them, and it was easy to just paddle along and forget until suddenly you'd hit one. We went downstream in record time, but it was hard work coming back. We were exhausted when we got to the landing place, and by the time we had put the canoe onto Jimmy's car, I was tired.

I had told Jimmy that even though I'd told my father I had four hundred dollars in the bank, he'd given me ten bucks. "Let's stop and get something to eat—and drink. I'm hot and thirsty," Jimmy said. "I haven't any money, but you have, haven't you?"

"Well, yes. You mean you want me to treat you?"

We were in the car and Jimmy glanced at me sideways. "Sure. Why not? You're the one with the dough."

"I've never treated a boy before. It's usually the other way around." I felt embarrassed. I'm not stingy, but I felt funny about it.

"Don't, if you don't want to," he said indifferently.

"I don't mind, except . . ."

"Except what?"

"Never mind." I didn't want to say that if I was his girl it would be different. He took other girls to the movies, not just me, and he went out with other girls. It bugged me that he was using me for the race because I was good at it—and now this.

But we stopped at a pizza place, and we had grinders and sodas and played the jukebox. I gave him my ten dollars to pay, and he carefully counted out the change to give back to me. "Here you are, down to the last penny," Jimmy said.

"You think I'm cheap, don't you?" I asked when we were back in the car.

"No, that's not it."

"Then what is it?"

"You're OK." He was evasive. "I like you. I think we could be good friends."

I didn't know any more than I did before. If

he really liked me, he sure didn't show it so I could recognize it.

My father was home when I got there. He looked tired and lonely sitting by himself at the kitchen table, eating cold leftovers. I looked at his plate and said, "Do you want me to fix you something decent to eat?"

He gave me a weak smile. "No, thanks. I'm capable of cooking, but I'm not very hungry. How was your canoeing on the river?"

"We're doing pretty good. I don't think we'll ever win a race, but we're not bad."

"Don't decide beforehand that you can't win. That's no way to go into a race."

"I thought you didn't want me to be competitive," I told him. Although I wasn't sure I wanted to, I sat down at the table with him.

"If you're racing, you have to be. I meant it in a different way. Always wanting to beat people in the normal course of your life. One-upmanship we call it. Like—"

"Like what?"

"Nothing, forget it." His elbows were resting on the table. With his head between his hands, he looked as if he hadn't slept for weeks.

"I know what you were going to say."

He glanced up at me curiously. "If you do, forget it anyway."

"You were going to say like Mrs. Craig." I

102

could tell by the look on his face. Besides she *was* pushy. I expected him to get angry, but he just sat there, staring into space.

"Yes, I was," he said finally. He straightened up in his chair and faced around toward me. "She's a very competitive woman, that's her problem. I'll tell you something, Melissa, and maybe you'll understand things better. Marilyn always measures herself against other women, instead of valuing herself and having her own goals. And she doesn't understand anything about friendship. I'm not putting all the blame on her; I was a fool. I started out being helpful to her in her work, in what she was doing, honest to God, as a friendly act. But she was after something else. She was jealous of your mother, your mother's life, and she doesn't understand a man wanting to help her, to just be friendly, without wanting more. One thing led to another . . . and I tell you I was stupid." He shook his head despairingly. "I thought if I told you a little bit about how it happened, you'd understand more. You wouldn't be so angry."

"I'm not that angry," I said, hoping it was true. "What I don't understand is how you can say you loved Mommy when you left to be with Mrs. Craig."

He looked crushed. "I didn't love Mrs. Craig," he said savagely; "it was just an infatuation. You're too young to understand, Melissa." He got up from the table. "You want to watch some TV?" he asked.

"OK." We went into the TV room and we sat together on the sofa. I felt closer to him than I had in a long time, but he had no idea of how much I did know. He had just wanted to sleep with Mrs. Craig. I wasn't too young to figure that one out. And it only proved what I had known all along, that a boy was after what he could get. Yet, when I got sleepy and snuggled up against my father, and he put his arm around me, I felt a nice, soft warmth. It made me believe there had to be a lot more to loving, with a boy, than sex. I closed my eyes and thought about Jimmy Ferris; I wondered what it would be like if he was on the sofa with me instead of my father. I thought it would be very nice.

The canoe race was on Saturday, and my mother came home the Friday night before. When my father brought her home from the airport, she looked great. "I had a fine rest," she said after she had kissed me and given me presents from my grandmother and aunt. My aunt had crocheted a terrific hat for me, and my grandmother had sent me a plaid skirt and a blouse. "How did you and Dad get along?" she asked, when we were in her room while she was unpacking and Dad was downstairs.

"Fine. We missed you, but . . . well, it was good for us to be alone for a bit."

She gave me an odd look. "I guess it was," she said after a few minutes. I had the feeling she wanted to ask me what we had talked about, but I was glad she decided not to. "It was good for me to get away." She took a skirt out of her suitcase and hung it up. When she turned to me her face had a determined look. "I think I can see things a little more objectively. It did me good."

"I'm glad." Impulsively I gave her a hug. I wanted to know so much that she could tell me, but I knew I would never ask: What was it like to fall in love? How did you know if you were in love? What if you were attracted to a boy—Jimmy Ferris—but you didn't know how he felt about you? How could you make him like you? I knew what she would say: "Wait until you're older, you'll find out for yourself." But you could make awful mistakes finding out for yourself.

"I'm going to bed early tonight," I said, "to be ready for the race tomorrow."

Saturday morning was cloudy and muggy. It was the kind of day when you don't feel like doing anything except floating in cool water. "It may clear up by this afternoon," my father said.

"Are you going to watch the race?" I asked my parents.

"We'll wait at the finish line," my father said.

"We could walk along the river," my mother suggested. "But it'll be awfully hot and buggy," she added.

They decided to wait at the finish line, which was just as well, I thought. Having them watch along the way would make me nervous.

Jimmy picked me up at around a quarter past twelve. The race was to start at one. He wore a sleeveless white shirt and bathing trunks. He had gotten very tan over the summer, and he looked great. After I put a pullover on over my bathing suit, we took off. There were a lot more canoes entering the race than I had expected, and the people in them weren't all kids. A few looked real old.

There were at least thirty canoes, and we were to leave in groups of five. The river wasn't wide enough to have everyone leave at once, so the winner wasn't going to be the canoe who reached the end first, but the one who did it in the shortest time. Second and third place would be figured the same way—by time.

There was quite a crowd to watch the start. I felt an unexpected thrill when the first five set off and everyone cheered. When Jimmy grabbed my hand, I could tell by his face that he felt the same way I did. I was glad he had asked me to go in with him. "All our hard work was worth it," Jimmy said, his eyes shining. "I don't even care if we win or not; it's terrific being here."

We watched the first five, and then the second, go down the river. The canoes looked beautiful, and in the hazy light—it was still very muggy—the river looked mysterious, kind of unreal. We left with the third group. I think we were the youngest. The others were older teenagers, except for one middle-aged couple, parents of kids I knew in school. "Just take it easy," Jimmy warned me. "Don't knock yourself out in the beginning."

We all lined up, and when the whistle blew, we took off. I could hear the cheers from the shore, and in spite of Jimmy's warning, we worked for speed. The water was relatively smooth for the first quarter mile or so; it was a good place to make time. When you got to the streams and currents where the rocks were, you couldn't just take long strokes ahead. With so many canoes in the water I didn't know what was going to happen. A canoe could get caught in between some of those rocks, or you could get bumped and be turned around, or turned over.

It was exciting. We passed a canoe that had started ahead of us. It must have flipped. One of the paddlers was in the water, scrambling to get back into the canoe. He didn't look as if he was in trouble, but we couldn't have stopped anyway. We'd picked up a current and were really going fast.

"I'm going to keep to the left," Jimmy called out to me. I nodded my head. I could see a few canoes bunched up to our right, so that made sense. Some of the people watching had followed a path along the river, but we were now on a stretch where that path was far above on a high cliff. We could hear voices up there, but we couldn't see anyone. It was weird.

"Don't get too close to the shore," I yelled back to Jimmy. I could see a patch of weeds ahead, and I didn't want us to get tangled up in that mess. I don't know if Jimmy didn't hear me, or if it was too late, but the side of the canoe hit a rock, and before I knew what was happening, I was in the water. I'm a good swimmer and I wasn't scared, except I didn't like the weeds. Ahead of me, Jimmy, also in the water, had hold of the boat, and was calling something back to me I couldn't hear. I swam a few strokes in his direction. Then I was caught. My leg was tangled up in the weeds and I couldn't pull myself out.

"Jim, I'm caught," I yelled to him. I could see that he was trying to get back into the boat, and I was afraid he didn't hear me. Suddenly there were some waves, I guess from the other canoes, and I was swamped. I went under and came up, trying to find a rock to cling to, but all I could grasp was more weeds.

Then I got scared. I was only five or six feet from shore, but I could have been in the middle of the ocean. I was stuck. "Jim . . . Jimmy . . . help, help . . ." I was yelling as loudly as I could, but I felt my voice was coming out in a hoarse whisper. I was going to drown. I was sure of it. I tried to keep my face out of the water, and I tried to pull the weeds from my leg, but I was getting exhausted, and I could feel my heart thumping wildly.

My eyes must have been closed when I felt a strong arm around me, holding me up. "Just keep your head up," Jimmy said. "Stop fighting. I'll get you loose." I don't know what he did, or how he did it, but in a few seconds I was being pulled to the shore and I lay panting on a bed of dirt. "Sit up." Jimmy sat me up, and pushed my head down between my knees. In a couple of minutes I threw up. Mostly water. He helped me rise and we went over to some grass and sat down.

"Where's the canoe?" I finally asked.

"Downstream I guess. Someone will get it. Are you OK?"

I looked at him, I mean right at him, for the first time. Everything had been hazy before. "Yes. I'm OK. Jimmy . . . you saved my life. I would have drowned. I don't know what to say. . . ."

"Don't say anything," he said gruffly. Then he grinned. "Did you think I'd go on and leave you there? I didn't do anything special."

I tried to be as light about it as he was. "Don't you think I'm special?"

He gave me a quick glance. "As a matter of fact I do."

Then I thought about the race. "After all our hard work . . . Jimmy, I feel terrible. And your canoe, I hope it's OK."

"It wasn't your fault. Just one of those things." He looked around. It was quite pretty where we were sitting; there was a carpet of grass surrounded by trees. "It's nice here."

"Shouldn't we go down, to get your boat?"

"I like it here."

We were sitting close. I leaned over toward him. "I should give you a kiss for saving my life."

"I wouldn't object." I kissed him lightly on the mouth and he kissed me back. I thought he was going to kiss me again, a real kiss, and he looked as if he wanted to. But instead, he stood up. I looked up at him standing there, staring out at the water. I was really hurt by the way he had gotten up so abruptly.

"You don't like me. do you?" I said.

He turned around and faced me. He was scowling. "I saved your life, didn't I? Listen, Melissa, I'm not going to be another boy you go with and drop. We can be friends, and that's it." He said it as if it had been on his mind for a long time.

"That *I* drop? You've got it all wrong. You boys think you can do anything you want and get away with it." I was furious and frustrated. First he had saved me and now he was rejecting me. I couldn't bear it. "You think a girl should be grateful to go out with you. You're the ones who take advantage, who are out to get what you can. Friends? That gives me a laugh. I am grateful that you saved my life, but I guess you picked the wrong girl to help you out with your race. I'm sorry I messed it up."

"So that's what you think. That I just needed you to help in the race? There were a lot of people I could have asked. People who were probably more experienced than you."

"I'm sorry you didn't ask them. You might have won, instead of my ruining it for you."

"Come on, let's go," he said abruptly. "This is a boring conversation."

I watched him start to climb up the steep hillside to the path above. I was in a rage and hurt. If he had only really kissed me instead of turning away. I wished I didn't have to follow him up the path. I never wanted to see him again, and yet, when he turned around and called to me to come on, I would have given anything to have him take me in his arms and really kiss me. Friends? How could we ever be friends?

We trudged along the path that followed the river downstream, and we were soon met by two of the men monitoring the race. They practically cheered when they saw us, they were so relieved. "We've got your empty boat," one of them said, "and we were coming back to look for you two. You gave us quite a scare. What happened?"

Jimmy told them although he didn't mention that he had saved my life. I added that to the story. "Good work." Both men patted Jimmy on the back. "We're sure glad to see you two," they said.

Fortunately my parents hadn't known that our empty boat had been picked up downstream; they'd have panicked. They were surprised to see us walking up to where everyone was waiting at the finish line. We repeated our story again, but this time I left out the lifesaving part. It would only have upset them. "Too bad after all your hard work," my dad said.

"As long as they're all right, it doesn't matter," was my mother's response. "There'll be more races for them."

Jimmy excused himself quickly and went off, muttering that he had to get his canoe. My father looked after him, surprised. "I was going to ask him if he wanted to go out with us."

"Where are we going?" I asked.

My father shrugged. "I don't know. . . . I

112

thought we could drive out someplace nice for dinner."

"He wouldn't have come," I said.

"Did you two have a fight?" my mother asked.

"Not exactly. Maybe sort of." I honestly didn't know if we had had a fight or not. I did know that when I was with Jimmy I never behaved as I wanted to. The way he had saved me had been terrific, but I had sounded pretty ungrateful afterward. I couldn't figure that boy out and it was driving me nuts.

My parents did drive out to a country inn for dinner, but all the time I kept thinking how super it would have been if Jimmy had been along.

Chapter Eight

A COUPLE OF WEEKS LATER, ANABEL AND I were sunning ourselves in her backyard. "How come you don't see Jimmy Ferris anymore?" Anabel asked me.

"We just saw each other for the canoe race. We never went together." I bent over to examine my legs. One of them was peeling.

"You saw each other almost every day. I'd call that going together." She looked at me with that amused smile of hers. "What did he do that made you drop him?"

I gave her a grin. "He saved my life." We both laughed. "As a matter of fact *I* didn't drop *him*. He said we could just be friends. Kiss of death."

"What's wrong with being friends?"

"Come on, Anabel. You know as well as I do, if a boy says let's be friends, you've got to be a creep. I mean if you're at all attractive, he's going to want to be more than friends. That's just a polite way of saying 'Get lost.'"

"I don't think so." Anabel spoke slowly. She lifted herself up to straighten the blanket we were both lying on. We had on bikini bathing suits, and her legs were smooth and tan; they weren't peeling at all. I rubbed my legs again with suntan lotion, and turned over onto my stomach. "He may really want to be friends," she said.

"Well, I'm not interested."

"I think you really like him."

"Maybe I do and maybe I don't." Anabel didn't know that I thought about him all the time. Soon after the race, we'd met in the village. He'd come over and spoken to me in a friendly way, as if nothing had happened between us. But he didn't say anything about seeing me. When he left he just said, "See you around. If you're not scared we can go out in the canoe again sometime."

"I'm not scared," I told him.

But that was all. I kept hoping he'd call me, but so far he hadn't. Every time I went into the village, I hoped I'd see him. A couple of times I saw him drive by in his car and he waved, but that was all. Even though I thought he'd just used me for the race, I hoped that wasn't it. But what was I to think now? The race was over and so was Jimmy Ferris.

"When you're alone with Peter, what do you talk about?" I asked Anabel.

"Everything. We talk about ourselves, books, our parents, some of our friends. Sometimes we talk about the future."

"Do you ever talk about me?"

Anabel laughed. "Sometimes. Peter thinks you put yourself down—the way you think every boy has an ulterior motive."

"I think most boys do. Maybe Peter doesn't. But that doesn't make me think less of myself, just less of them," I said.

"No." Anabel sat up. Her face was serious. "Don't you see, if you think a boy wants something from you, then you believe he doesn't like you for what you are? That's putting yourself down."

"Mmmm . . ." I didn't say anything more. This was something I had to think about when I was alone.

A few days after that I was out running. When I went past Jimmy's house, he was on the porch and he came out and joined me. It was just like the last time he had done that. He fell into step alongside me as if it was something he did every day. I didn't say a word and when he smiled at me I smiled back. We ran about three miles, but instead of going to the reservoir Jimmy turned in to a path in the woods, and I went along. Running always made me feel terrific. It was exciting to have Jimmy join me that way without any plan, and you can't be angry with someone on a super day when you're running together.

When the path ended in some woods and bushes we stopped, both of us hot and breathing hard. "Kiss of death," I said.

"What?" Jimmy was panting.

"Stopping. We should keep on going till we get home."

"I know, but I felt like stopping. Let's sit down."

We found an open space and some grass and we sat down. He sat, but I stretched out. The sun on my face felt good.

"You still mad at me?" Jimmy gave me a half smile, but his eyes were serious.

"You were the one who got mad."

"You're darned right, I did. You said some pretty mean things. I thought you and I were friends."

"Maybe we have different meanings for the word," I told him. I was looking up at the sky, but the sun in my eyes made me close them. Suddenly I felt Jimmy's face close and he was kissing me. Real kisses.

I wanted to pull him down to me and hold him tight. In spite of our both being hot, he had a clean, fresh smell like he was part of the woods. But I pushed him away gently and sat up. "I thought you didn't want to get involved," I said.

He gave me a hurt look. "Don't take everything I say so literally. I wasn't going out of my way to get involved, but looking at you lying there, I wanted to kiss you, that's all."

"Just a passing fancy?"

"Do you have to put a name on everything? Can't you just take things as they come. Why are you so worried?"

"I have reason to be." I couldn't believe what was happening to me. I sat there dying to have him hold me, kiss me, to kiss him, but I was afraid. Afraid he'd let me down, afraid I'd be sick with shame if he was just casual, if this wasn't terribly important to him. Jimmy, of all people, who said he had to truly count on a girl before he wanted to make love. Had he been putting on an act, too? How could I ever know when a boy was telling me the truth?

"You're letting what your father did color everything," Jimmy said, as if reading my thoughts. "You're so mixed up you don't even trust yourself. Come on, let's go." He held out his hand and pulled me up. He did that all the time, just ended a conversation abruptly.

We didn't run home; we walked, but we hardly spoke. I felt terribly depressed, thinking that everything was going to end this way for me. Jimmy gave me a kind of hopeless, bewildered look when he left me. "You know you're not the only one in the world who doesn't like to be rejected," he said, and before I could answer, he ran up on his porch and was gone. I walked home the rest of the way alone, feeling as though I were at the bottom of a pit. It seemed as if Jimmy and I were always misunderstanding each other. I never really understood what he felt, and he didn't see that I needed him to make himself clear.

I was in an awful depression after that. I didn't even want to talk to Anabel about it.

Then something really weird happened. It was Sunday night, almost nine-thirty, when the phone rang. I was watching television with my parents, and I was surprised when Mom said it was for me. I'd talked to Anabel earlier, so I couldn't imagine who would be calling me.

"Melissa, this is Jimmy." His voice sounded agitated. "I'm at the drugstore, Park's. Can you come down and meet me?"

"Now?" I was stunned.

"Yes, now. It's important, please."

"It's so late. I don't know. . . ."

"It's only half past nine. It's an emergency. I'll wait for you at Mary's Coffee Shop, OK? Hurry up."

I said OK but when I hung up I thought, I'm stupid. He left me hanging in midair. Now he calls up like that and I go running. I am a darned fool. I could have kicked myself for saying yes, but he did sound very upset. I wondered what my parents would think when I said I was going out now.

Predictably they both said, "It's so late."

"I'm just going down to meet Jimmy. I'll be back soon."

It was a bright night with an almost-full moon. The air smelled fresh from Sunday's newly mowed lawns—a regular routine on our street. I like walking at night, and I got excited about seeing Jimmy, besides being wildly curious about why he had called me. My feelings for Jimmy went back and forth like crazy. A few minutes before, I'd been angry with him for calling and at myself for running to meet him, but now I felt shot through with a thrilling sense of adventure, mad about Jimmy for calling me out.

He was waiting outside Mary's, and he really looked upset. He was walking up and down nervously. "Oh boy, am I glad to see you," he said, taking me by the arm and leading me inside. He headed right for a booth way in the back where we'd have privacy.

When we got inside I saw that he had a big bruise across his cheek and his left hand was bandaged. "What happened?" He looked terrible, pale under his suntan.

He sat down before he answered, and I sat opposite him. "I smashed up my mother's car." He leaned back and closed his eyes for a minute. "I guess I'm lucky I'm alive. The cop said it was a miracle."

"Oh, Jimmy. Are you all right? When did it happen? Tell me."

"Let's order first. What do you want?"

We both ordered sodas, and Jimmy ordered a sandwich. "If I can eat it . . ." he said. "I haven't eaten for ages."

"Where are your parents?"

"They're away. They went to see my brothers; they're both in Arizona. Thank goodness they're away. It'll give me a chance to get the car fixed I hope, before they get back."

"So what happened?"

"I don't know. I was driving along Route 169 this afternoon, in the middle of the afternoon, and all of a sudden there was this huge tree in front of me—you know, something gigantic,"—he made a large circle of his arms to show me—"and I was heading right into it and I couldn't stop. I smashed up the front of the car and the left fender. I tried to pull around, but it was too late. I did hardly anything to myself. Hit my face against something and sprained my wrist. It's the car I'm worried about. My mother will have a fit."

"But why did it happen? I mean in the middle of the day?" I looked at him suspiciously. "You weren't drinking, were you?"

"No, the first thing the cop did was to smell

121

my breath. He thought I must have dozed off. Maybe I did. I haven't been sleeping much." He leaned across the table. "Melissa, you think you can help me?"

"What can I do?" I was genuinely surprised.

"Lend me some money. The car's going to cost six hundred bucks to get fixed. I've got about three hundred. I thought you could lend me the other three hundred. If I get the car fixed before my parents get home, life will be much easier. I have an awful feeling they don't have collision insurance on that car. It's three years old, and I'm pretty sure they dropped it; it was so expensive. Can you do it? I'll pay you back maybe by the end of the summer, but positively at Christmas. I always get money then. Can you?" His eyes were searching my face eagerly.

I was shocked. I didn't know what to say. Three hundred dollars. That was a lot of money. I only had four hundred in the bank, and I was saving to buy a new stereo that would cost around five or six hundred. If I gave him three hundred I'd only have a hundred left. And why me? Why did he ask me? I didn't want to meet his eyes, I felt so uncomfortable.

"I don't know," I mumbled. "I don't know if I have three hundred . . ."

"You told me you had four hundred dollars in the bank," he said softly. "I'll pay it back;

I'll even pay you interest if you want. Whatever the bank pays you."

"It's not that . . ." Then I did look at him. "Why me? Why are you asking me? I mean you must have close friends. . . ."

"I thought you were my friend." He said it quietly, but there was something in his voice that made me wince and feel as though I had pulled a chair out from under him, or done something awful that hurt him.

"Well, yes, in a way," I hedged. "But I mean we weren't really friends."

"I thought we were. OK, never mind. I'll figure out something. I don't want to talk you into anything. Let's see . . . I don't want to go to any of my parents' friends. . . . Off hand I can't think of anyone with money in the bank, but I'll find someone . . ." his voice trailed off.

"You don't understand." I rested my elbows on the table and held my head with my hands. The expression on his face was making me feel a little sick, but I wanted him to understand. "I mean I was never your girl; you know what I mean. It's not like we were close. You just wanted me for the race; I know that. And now . . . well, to tell you the truth, it makes me feel like I'm someone you can use when you want to. You know—call me out of the blue because you knew I had some money in the bank. It makes me feel funny."

"I said forget it." He had pulled his face together, and he was stern. "I don't want your money, and I don't need you for a friend. You don't know what it means, anyway. You have no idea, none."

"Thanks. Just because I'm not a sucker, you don't like it. I'm sorry you had an accident, I really am, but it's pretty peculiar for you to expect me to take care of it." My voice was angry, but my feelings were actually more complicated.

"I don't expect anything of you, anything at all. Come on, let's go." Half his sandwich was on his plate, but he picked up the check and stood up. I felt I had started something I couldn't stop, as if someone else was pulling the strings, making me act and speak in a certain way. But my feelings were all different; I felt terrible.

I followed him outside. He barely said good night and walked away. I was tempted to run after him, to put my arms around him and tell him he could have all my money, but I turned toward my own house. I was crying, and I wasn't sure why.

My parents were still up when I came home, and my mother immediately saw that I had been crying. "Do you want to tell us what happened?" she asked.

"Not really." But I looked at them both and burst into tears.

"What's the matter? Did you have a fight with Jimmy?"

"Kind of," I sobbed. Then I pulled up my head and wiped my face with my sleeve which brought an annoyed look to my mother's face. That expression of hers, looking at me as if I had done something terribly vulgar, set me off. When she said, "Use a tissue," I yelled at her, "I don't want a tissue."

I faced them both. "It's all your fault, the two of you. You haven't taught me anything," I yelled. "I don't know how to act with boys, I don't know anything about people. You two say one thing and do another; you say you love each other and all that stuff, but you don't. You fight. Daddy goes off with someone else; Mommy picks up and goes away. One minute you're all lovey-dovey, and the next Mommy's crying and Daddy takes off. How can anyone expect me to know how to behave?" I wailed and sobbed and hid my head in my arms.

When my father put his hand on my shoulder, it felt like a shot of electricity. I shook him away and started to get up to leave. He gave me a gentle push back into the chair. "When you stop crying we can talk."

"I don't want to talk," I mumbled.

"Perhaps it will be better to wait till tomorrow." My mother sounded apprehensive.

"I think we should talk about it right now," my father said firmly.

"I don't care what you say; I don't want to talk about anything." I looked at him defiantly. "You can't order me to talk. You can't order me to do anything. For all I know you could leave tomorrow, and I'd never see you again. And you know what? I wouldn't care either."

"Melissa!" My mother's voice was choked.

My father was white and tight-lipped. I braced myself against a slap from him. I felt we had reached a point from which there was no turning back. In two minutes I had shot up to someone ten feet tall. My father and I might live in the same house for years to come, but I knew then we would never be close the way we used to be. I would never be his little girl again. I knew then, standing there facing him, that it wasn't only what he had done to my mother that I resented, but what he had done to me. He had betrayed me. He had turned me into a confused, cynical person, and I hated him for it.

"I'm going to bed," I announced, and before they could stop me I went up to my room and banged my door shut.

My room was my refuge. I felt it was the only place in the world where no one could bother me, where I was in charge. Everything in it was mine: a few stuffed animals I had hung on to over the years, shells I had gathered on various beaches, necklaces hung up around my mirror, pictures of me on a horse and riding a small tricycle, a beautiful turtle I had made in a craft class, pillows, a pile of sample fabrics my mother had once given me that at some time I intended to use for pillows, an old fur skin. If I could only live in this room and never go out of it, I'd be all right. But the thought of having to face my parents, to sit and have meals with them, to have my mother's anxious eyes watching me, and to look at my father's grim face was too much. I kept thinking about Jimmy. What was he going to do? I kept telling myself that surely he must have someone else from whom he could borrow the money, but I couldn't get his hurt and reproachful eyes out of my mind.

When I heard my parents come upstairs and their low voices talking, I quickly turned off my lights. I didn't want them to come in to try to talk to me. I got undressed in the dark and got into bed. Before I fell asleep I made up my mind that first thing in the morning I was going over to Anabel's. Maybe I would stay with her for a few days until things calmed down. Until I calmed down. Even as I curled up in bed, I could feel my heart racing.

Chapter Nine

THE NEXT MORNING I STAYED IN BED UNTIL I heard both my parents leave the house. When I went downstairs, I found a note from my mother saying she'd be home around two o'clock. Before I even drank my orange juice, I called up Anabel to tell her I was coming over. I wasn't very hungry, but I nibbled on some cold chicken I'd found in the fridge and drank a glass of milk. Anabel had said to hurry up because she had an errand to do, but that I could do it with her.

I put on a pair of shorts and a jersey. It was beginning to get hot out already, so I took a bathing suit and a towel with me. Anabel was waiting for me on her porch.

"I have to go over to Bill's house," she said. "What's the matter? You sounded in a state."

"I am. I'll tell you about it. But I don't want to go over to Bill's. What are you going there for?"

"I'm taking care of his dogs. He's away with his family. I have to feed them and take them out. No one's home. Come on, you can help me. Sometimes it's hard to manage the two of them."

I looked at her in surprise. "Why are you taking care of his dogs? Aren't you going with Peter anymore? What's going on? You didn't tell me you were going with Bill." I was really hurt, and I still didn't want to go to Bill's house even if no one was there.

"I'm *not* going with Bill. Don't jump to conclusions so fast. I'm just taking care of his dogs. He asked me to and I said I would. We're friends. It's no big deal; it's just for a week. He hates putting them in a kennel, and besides that's so expensive for two of them. I go over in the morning and take them out and feed them, usually earlier than this, then later in the middle of the day, and then in the evening I take them out again. They're pretty good, except I hate meeting another dog when I have the two of them on their leashes; they get so excited. That's why I'm glad you're with me." She was walking while she was talking, and I was walking with her.

But I stopped. "It sounds like an awful lot to

129

me. I didn't know you and Bill were so chummy. Doesn't Peter mind?"

"Come on." Anabel tugged on my arm. "We're good friends, I told you that. Peter knows, he doesn't mind. Why should he?"

I followed along silently for a bit. Then I told her.

"I'm in a mess. I don't know what to do." I blurted out the whole story about Jimmy and his car and his asking me for the money, and about the fight I'd had with my parents. "What do you think?" I asked when I'd finished. "I suppose you think I should give Jimmy the money?"

Anabel looked at me critically. We were outside Bill's house and we could hear the dogs barking at the door. "That's up to you," she said. "It's your money; I'm not going to tell you what to do." Anabel had a key, and when she opened the door, the two black Labradors jumped all over her and licked her face. I was afraid they would knock her down, but when she told them to stay, they sat down and wagged their tails. She put on their leashes and we each took one and went to a path in the woods in back of Bill's house.

"They're awfully good, aren't they?" Anabel looked at the dogs admiringly. "I like them."

"Bill has them well trained," I said. But my

mind was on Jimmy. I kept wondering what he was doing and if he'd gotten the money for his mother's car. Anabel and I walked the dogs for around twenty minutes, until they had sniffed all the trees and done what they had to do.

When we got back to the house, I watched Anabel get their dishes, measure out dry food for each, and then split a can of dog meat between the two. She was very careful and efficient about giving each the same amount. "It's quite a job, isn't it?" I said.

Anabel shrugged. "I don't mind. I like animals. And I like Bill," she added with a grin. "He'd do the same for me."

"Would he?"

Anabel gave me a sharp look. "Of course he would. I told you; he and I are friends."

I gave a deep sigh. I was sitting on a stool watching her, and I wound my legs around the stool. "I guess it's hard for me to believe that a boy can be a real friend."

"You've never given one a chance; you're too suspicious." Anabel said. She had her back to me, so I couldn't see her face; but there was a note of impatience in her voice.

"You're my best friend, but you think I'm a creep, don't you?" I said morosely.

She was waiting for the dogs to finish their food before she filled their pans with water. "No, I don't," she said slowly. "I think you're

131

confused. I can understand why," she added hastily. "You have reason. But I think you've got to get over it."

"I know," I said. "I know you're right."

I suppose I had known from the minute I had left Jimmy what I had to do. But it wasn't easy. I wondered if other girls my age had to make big decisions like this on their own. I only had four hundred dollars in the bank, and to take out three hundred to lend to a boy, who wasn't even my boyfriend, was a big thing. Under the circumstances I wasn't going to ask my parents what to do. They were in a mess of their own, and they weren't so great about handling their own problems.

I waited for Anabel to finish taking care of the dogs. When we left the house and she had locked the door, we walked up the street silently. At the corner I said, "I think I'll go over and see if Jimmy's home."

I looked directly at Anabel. Her eyes were very bright. Without a word she put her arms around me and gave me a great bear hug. "I'm glad, I'm very glad," she whispered. She made me feel like crying.

Jimmy's house was in the opposite direction from where Anabel and I lived. I walked toward his street slowly. The sun was getting hot, but the street was shaded with trees, and it was pretty with the sun coming through the leaves. I passed two little kids, a girl and a boy, riding their tricycles up and down the sidewalk in front of their house. They were having a wonderful time. They both said "Hi" to me, and for some reason that made me feel good. I didn't even know them.

I felt nervous and shaky as I approached Jimmy's house. I had never done anything like this before, and I expected Jimmy to still be very angry with me. His house was in the middle of the block, a white clapboard house with black shutters. Before I got there I almost turned around to run home. I could so easily let it go. I'd already said no to him, and I could let it stay that way.

I don't know what pushed me to go on. But then I did know. Maybe it was the look of relief in Anabel's eyes when I said I was going to Jimmy's house, her expression telling me that I hadn't failed her expectation of me. It hit me that Jimmy must be thinking the same thing: I was a creep who couldn't be anyone's friend. He had said he wanted a girl he could count on and he had turned to me. He must have had some hope that I could be that girl, be generous and giving. That was pretty terrific. He must have really believed that he could count on me. Suddenly, I felt as if I were a big person like my mother. Someone who thought enough of herself to be trusting, not afraid to give. I hadn't realized how fantastic my mother was, taking my father back. She wasn't a dope at all.

I quickened my steps. That freckle-faced Jimmy didn't know it, but he was the one doing me the favor. I'd show him, show myself, that I could be a friend, no strings attached. I started to run. I felt great.

His house looked dark and empty, but I rang the bell. I could hear it ringing inside. I hope he's there, I thought. Please God, I don't want him to have done something awful because he didn't get the money.

After I rang a second time, Jimmy opened the door. I heaved a big sigh of relief. "I'm so glad to see you," I said.

His hair was all tousled and he looked sleepy. "What are you doing here?"

"Can't I come in?" I couldn't blame him for not being very cordial, but I didn't want to just stand there.

"I suppose so. I just got up. You want some coffee?"

I followed him into the kitchen. The sink was piled with dishes, but there was a pot of coffee on the stove. You could tell his parents had been away. Jimmy wasn't much of a house-keeper. He looked around at the mess.

"I don't mind," I told him.

Jimmy poured us each a cup of coffee. He put three lumps of sugar in his and put a bottle of milk on the table. "What's up?" he asked me when we were both sitting in the kitchen.

"I want to lend you the money," I said. "The three hundred dollars."

Jimmy raised his eyes to meet mine. They still looked sleepy, but had taken on a wary expression. "You do?" was all he said. I hadn't expected him to turn handsprings, he wasn't the type to whoop for joy, but I was a little annoyed by the way he kept looking at me. As if he'd heard, but he hadn't heard.

"Yes," I fairly shouted. "The three hundred dollars for your car. If you come with me, I'll go home and get my bankbook, and we can go to the bank. I'll give it to you."

He was beginning to wake up. "What made you change your mind? I mean you felt so funny about it yesterday. I can't say I don't want you to do me a favor—it is a favor, a big one—but I don't want you to do something you don't feel right about doing."

"I thought about it," I said. "Maybe I was just taken by surprise yesterday." I drank some of my coffee. "No, that's not the truth." How could I tell him that I hadn't thought of him as a friend? "Does it matter why I changed my mind?"

"Yes, to me it does. When you accept a favor, a big favor from someone, it's not terribly different from giving it. It kind of puts you under an obligation."

"You don't have to feel obligated to me.

135

Besides," I said with a grin, "you already saved my life. So we're even." It was too complicated to tell him that he had done me a big favor by asking me for the loan.

"Is that why you changed your mind?" Jimmy asked.

"No. I hadn't even thought of that until this minute. I think I have to change my mind about a lot of things. Lending you the money was only one of them. Come on, let's go."

"You're sure you want to do it?"

"Don't keep asking me. Don't you want the money?"

Jimmy came over to me and took my hand in both of his. "You're a true-blue friend," he said with mock drama, yet I knew he was serious.

"I want to be your friend," I said, equally serious.

We went back to my house, and I ran upstairs and got my bankbook. I was glad my mother still hadn't come home. Jimmy and I went straight to the bank. When we got inside, I felt funny having him with me, as if people were lookng at us, and when they saw me take the money, they'd think we were running away. The teller asked me if I wanted a check or cash, and I told him cash. He gave me two crisp one-hundred-dollar bills and the other hundred in twenties and tens. I had never seen a hundred-dollar bill before. It looked like nothing, like it couldn't buy anything.

Jimmy seemed nervous when I handed him the money. "Put it away," I told him. "Haven't you got a wallet?"

"Yes, sure I have." He pulled out a worn, old leather thing from his back pants pocket. The money looked so clean and new next to it.

"I should have a new wallet for so much money," he said with a sheepish grin.

Right from the bank we went to the body-repair shop where his mother's car was. "The guy wants half the money before he does any work," Jimmy explained. When I saw the car, I nearly had a fit. It looked awful. "You could have been killed," I said, gripping Jimmy's arm.

"I know." Jimmy grinned. "That's what the cop said."

I waited while Jimmy talked to the man who worked there, then gave him the money. Jimmy got a receipt and put it away in his wallet.

"I sure thank you," Jimmy said when we left. Suddenly I felt embarrassed. Somehow giving Jimmy the money made me feel closer to him; yet actually I wasn't any closer. He had still never asked me to be his girl friend. I felt peculiar, not knowing what we were to each other.

"Want to stop and have a soda?" Jimmy asked.

"No, thanks. I've got to go home." There was nothing I had to go home for, but I wanted to get away. I left him and walked home slowly, remembering that I still had my parents to deal with.

My mother was home when I got there. She was sitting out in the yard on a deck chair sunning herself. In a pair of white shorts and a sleeveless top, she looked like a kid, but even though she was lying back with her eyes closed, she had a little frown on her forehead. She didn't look relaxed.

She opened her eyes when she heard me. "I hope you're in a better mood today," she said.

"I am." I wanted to tell her about lending Jimmy the money and how thinking about her had helped me, but I felt embarrassed. After all, you can't tell your mother you'd been thinking she was kind of dopey—as far as my father was concerned anyway—and then say all of a sudden you've realized how terrific she was. "You OK?"

She looked at me, surprised. "Yeah, why do you ask?"

"You look tired."

"I am." She gave a deep sigh. When she

looked at me again even through her sunglasses I could see that her eyes looked teary. I was sure she had been crying.

"I'm sorry if I upset you last night," I said. "You and Dad."

"Thank you." She stretched out her hand and patted my arm. I was sitting on the grass by her chair. "You're a good girl. I wish your father and I weren't giving you such a hard time. Your father was very angry last night, angry and upset. You see," she said with a thin smile, "you hit where it hurt because a lot of what you said was true. I'm in a terrible muddle, and I don't know how to get out of it. I feel awful that you've been bearing the brunt of it. It isn't fair to you."

I sat back, stunned. I couldn't believe this was my mother talking to me this way. I mean my mother and I got along well, we were pretty close, but this was different. Her voice was so emotional. I had the feeling she was really in the pits and that she was turning to me for help—me, her fifteen-year-old daughter. For all the times I'd thought she was treating me like too much of a kid, now I felt scared that all of a sudden she was turning to me like I was a grown-up. It was weird.

"I'm OK Mom," I said. I wanted to tell her how just a short while before I'd been thinking of how terrific she was, but I felt shy. When I get mad I can say everything I feel, anything that comes into my head, but when it comes to saying something nice, I have a hard time. "I'm glad that Dad came home, and that it was OK with you. It was terrific of you to do it." At least I made a stab at saying it.

"Me, terrific? Oh Lord, I'm not, I'm not at all. I'm a mess. Don't you see, what you said last night was true? You said that for all you knew he might go out and never come back; that's on my mind all the time. I've been telling you I have to trust him. I know I do, but it's so hard. So terribly hard. I get so scared, I'm a wreck."

It was like seeing my mother for the first time. My mother. Kind of scatterbrained around the house, but like I said before, all put together and collected on her job. I never thought of my mother as being frightened or sad—you know, someone crawling under the covers to cry. Even when my father was away, and we were alone, she joked and laughed. I honestly was dumb enough to think she wasn't minding so much.

Naturally I thought about Jimmy and me. I know it sounds crazy to compare two kids— kids who've never even really made love— with people who've been married for almost twenty years, but I thought how awful I would feel if I didn't trust Jimmy. Once I lent him the money, I knew that I did trust him. I couldn't have done it otherwise. It was as if all my doubts had vanished when I did something that showed I trusted him, that we were friends.

"But you do trust Daddy," I said to my mother. "You wouldn't have taken him back if you didn't. It's scary only when you're not trusting him—like lying in the dark and imagining there are peculiar shapes and noises outside. I've decided I'm going to stop thinking he's going to leave again. I'm going to concentrate on that, and after a while I'll stop thinking it."

"Can you do that?" She had taken off her sunglasses, and her eyes were wide. "Can you just make up your mind like that?"

"Why not? I can, I know I can. The way I made up my mind this morning—about Jimmy. I decided I had to trust him. If he thought of me as a friend I had to be that friend. If I didn't I was being a creep, using that as an excuse not to help him." I told my mother about taking my money out of the bank and lending it to him.

"Three hundred dollars? Will he pay it back?" Mom was upset.

"He will. I know he will. I'm not going to worry about it. Mom, you've said it to me many times. If you can't trust your friends, if a person can't count on you, then you have no friends."

My mother smiled. "I know. Mellie, I'm proud of you."

"And Dad's your friend. You've told me that too, don't forget it."

She really looked better when she got up to go inside to take a shower. She put on a long caftan and looked awfully pretty when my father came home. He seemed pleased and even forgot to scold me for yelling at him the night before.

Chapter Ten

I DIDN'T HEAR FROM JIMMY FOR A FEW DAYS, and all my doubts came flooding back: now that he had the money he didn't need me anymore, and I'd never see him again. I was miserable. Every time the phone rang I went running. I alternated between not wanting to leave the house for fear I'd miss his call, and deciding that I wasn't going to hang around waiting to hear from him.

My mother knew I was in a state, and she easily guessed the reason. "Why don't you call him?" she asked me. It was about a week since I'd given him the money and my mother and I had had our little talk. "He may be shy about calling you."

I shook my head. "No. I wouldn't know what to say, and I think he should call me. That is if he wants to see me. Maybe he doesn't give a hang about me."

"I don't believe that," she said. She smiled. "Remember what you told me: you've got to believe in yourself and the person you care about. We women better stick together," she added with a grin.

A little more than a week had passed before he did phone and ask if I wanted to go canoeing with him. I hesitated for a few seconds, thinking that I shouldn't say yes and let him think he could call me at the last minute that way; but then I said, "Sure, I'd love to go." I decided it was silly to play games. I wanted to see him so it would have been stupid for me to say no.

He said he'd pick me up at twelve o'clock, and we agreed that I'd bring sandwiches for lunch and he'd bring sodas. It was only ten o'clock when he called, so the next two hours dragged. I made tuna fish sandwiches and wrapped them up in wax paper. Then, deciding I was hungry, I ate one of them and had to open another can of tuna to make more. But only half an hour had gone by. I tried to read, but my mind kept wandering. Finally I changed the polish of my toenails and then sat worrying that it wouldn't be dry by the time he came.

Jimmy arrived at five minutes to twelve. He looked super, a lot better than when I had last seen him. "I've been working," he told me. "This is my first day off. I've been helping Mr. Larkin clear out the woods in back of his house. It was fun except when it got too buggy. But I made a lot of money. He really pays well, and if he gives me more work I'll be able to pay you back in no time. By the end of the summer for sure."

"That'll be great," I said, feeling guilty that I had had such bad thoughts about him. "When did you get the car? It looks terrific; you'd never know it was banged up."

"I got it late yesterday. Yeah, they did a good job. I'm sure relieved to have it back before my parents come home. They're due this weekend."

"Are you going to tell them?"

"Yes. So long as it's fixed, and I paid for it, they can't make a big fuss. Also maybe they have insurance. That would be fantastic."

"Then we'd both get our money back. I hope for your sake they do."

When we got to the river, I helped Jimmy get the canoe off the car and into the water. I hadn't been on the river since the race and the accident, and suddenly I felt nervous. I remembered struggling in the water.

I guess I turned pale. "What's the matter?" Jimmy asked me.

"Nothing. Come on."

Jimmy didn't say anything until we were in the canoe, going down the river. "Don't be scared," he said. "Nothing's going to happen. I wouldn't let you drown."

"How do you know? You might not always be able to save me."

"I know. I'd save you. Just trust good old Jimmy."

"How did you know I was scared?"

He laughed. "It was written all over your face. I can tell everything you're thinking. It shows."

"Oh boy, *that's* scary. I don't want you to know everything I'm thinking."

"You have bad thoughts?"

"Sometimes. Mostly private ones. Anyway, I don't think you do know." I laughed. "You probably wouldn't see me if you did."

"You have bad thoughts about me?"

"Sometimes."

He stopped paddling and let the boat drift, except to steer it away from the rocks. "Let's pull in to shore," he said. He steered the canoe into a small inlet, and we pulled it up on the land.

"You want to explore?" Jimmy asked.

"Sure."

The land was quite steep where we were, and after we climbed we came to a huge forest. There was nothing but trees as far as you could see—huge trees. Jimmy said maybe they were virgin growth. The ground underneath was thick with leaves and beautiful to walk on. We both took off our sneakers.

"Let's sit down," Jimmy whispered. I knew by his soft voice that he felt the same as I did; the silence was beautiful. He took my hand and led me to a place where the sun came through the trees. Jimmy sat hugging his knees, and I lay on my stomach beside him. We were both quiet.

After a bit he put out his hand and touched my hair. "Your hair is pretty in the sun," he said. "It has red glints in it."

My face was hidden in my arms, but I turned and smiled up at him. Then he bent down, and turned me over and kissed me. A real kiss.

I was surprised and I wasn't surprised. I think I knew when we docked the canoe that he wanted to do more than explore the woods. I sat up and said, "Jimmy."

"Come here and be close," he said, and held me in his arms.

I let him hold me, but I said, "I thought we were just friends."

"What do you mean, 'just' friends? Of course we're friends, real friends. I know it now; I wasn't sure for a long time."

"I don't know what you mean."

"I was never sure you were my friend. You were always so kind of suspicious and wary, like you didn't trust me. Sometimes you acted as if you thought I was a creep. I'm not one of those boys who just wants to make out—I told

147

you I really have to like a girl before I want to, you know, kiss her and stuff. I have to feel she's my friend."

"You feel that way now?"

"Yes." He kissed me again. "Don't you? You've got to be my friend." He grinned. "You wouldn't have lent me that money otherwise."

I felt funny when he said that, a little bit ashamed. I had never thought of friendship and being in love as part of a whole. I'd thought they were two different things. I put my arms around Jimmy and kissed him hard on the mouth. "I'm glad you're my friend," I said. "Very glad."

"Me too. I'm glad. I love you." We held each other close and kissed until we were out of breath. Once, when I opened my eyes and looked up at the sky, it was the bluest blue I had ever seen. I was very happy.

I hated saying good-bye to Jimmy. It was awful. I wanted to be with him all the time. I hated the thought of going home, being alone without him. I had never felt this way before about anyone. Loving someone, I thought, wasn't all joy. "I'll call you later," Jimmy said. "I have to work tomorrow, but we'll see each other soon."

We kissed again and again before I got out of his car, and I didn't even care if anyone saw us.

*   *   *

I floated into my house. Everything looked beautiful to me: a yellow bowl my mother had filled with daisies, the orange kettle on the stove, a basket of fresh spinach sitting on the kitchen counter. My mother came into the kitchen and looked at me curiously. "What happened to you?"

"Nothing. Why?"

"You look all starry-eyed. What did you and Jimmy do?" Her eyes were anxious.

"Nothing wrong, don't worry. I think I'm in love."

"You're much too young to be in love. There will be a lot of young men in your life before you truly fall in love."

She carried the spinach to the sink to wash it.

"That's what you think. I'll never love anyone the way I love Jimmy. You're the one who once said there's no love like the first love."

"I meant the first real love. That was your father for me. I had other boyfriends before, and I thought that was it—but it wasn't."

I noticed that she kept looking at the clock. "When's Dad coming home?" I asked.

"I don't know. He called to say he would be late." She had her back to me, but I could tell by her voice she was unhappy again.

I went over to her and put my arms around her. "Mom, you said you were going to stop worrying; you were going to trust him."

"I know. Saying and doing aren't always the same. She turned around to get a pot for the spinach. Her face was dark, the way it gets when she is worried.

"Are you and Dad friends?" I asked.

She gave me a quick, surprised look. "That's a funny question. To tell you the truth, I consider your father my best friend. Why do you think I put up with what he did? Why do you think I took him back?" Her eyes were fierce.

"I don't know. You haven't been very happy about it."

"No, I haven't, but that's my fault. I have to keep reminding myself that he is my friend. There's a lot more to our relationship than one infidelity. That was only sex, and that's not the most important thing between a husband and wife. I'm not putting it down. It is important, but it isn't everything. It is because we are friends, because we have so much going for us besides sex—talking to each other, a whole past of memories, our loving you, enjoying our house, our friends, just being with each other— I wasn't going to throw all that out because he suddenly had a physical attraction for someone else. If there were to be others, that would be different. I wouldn't tolerate that—that would mean our marriage wasn't working for him anymore."

"Then why do you still worry every time he's late?"

"Because that's human nature." She was almost yelling. "You can know something in your head, but your emotions don't get the message. I'll get over it," she said in a quieter voice. "I'm working on it."

I left her and went upstairs to my room. I wanted to think about Jimmy and me. My mother was wrong. I was going to love him forever because he was my friend—my best friend. I knew that no matter what happened, Jimmy would never hurt me. And once you have a best friend, you never stop loving that person. My mother knew that. She's the one who taught me that even when it hurts, you go on loving.

After a while I heard my father's car come into the driveway, and I breathed a sigh of relief. I stayed up in my room until my mother called me down for supper. When I came into the kitchen, where we ate, my mother's face was no longer dark. It seemed to me that working on her bad thoughts, like she said, was going to pay off. When the three of us sat down to eat, I felt nice and warm inside. Loving Jimmy made me feel closer to them, as if there was a new bond between us—as if I was taking first steps into their world, and that I'd begin to understand better what went on between them.

ABOUT THE AUTHOR

HILA COLMAN was born and raised in New York City and later attended Radcliffe College. She began writing books for young people after writing stories and articles for magazines. Ms. Colman writes nearly every day and her mind is always a few ideas ahead of her typewriter. She is the author of numerous award-winning books stemming from an interest in the problems of adolescence. Her books often explore family relationships, which she feels directly affect young people's attitudes and lives.

Besides writing, Hila Colman enjoys traveling and is active in politics, serving on several town committees and as a trustee of her local library. She makes her home in Bridgeport, Connecticut, and has two sons, both of whom are married.